The Lady in Red
An Anthology of Short Stories and Other Works

J.G. Barrie

J.G. Barrie

Copyright © 2018 J.G. Barrie
All rights reserved. No part of this work may be reproduced or transmitted in any form or by any means, electronic or mechanical, without permission of the author.
The stories in this collection are fictional. Some may have been influenced by actual events but names have been changed. Others are historical fiction based on real characters and events available in the public domain.

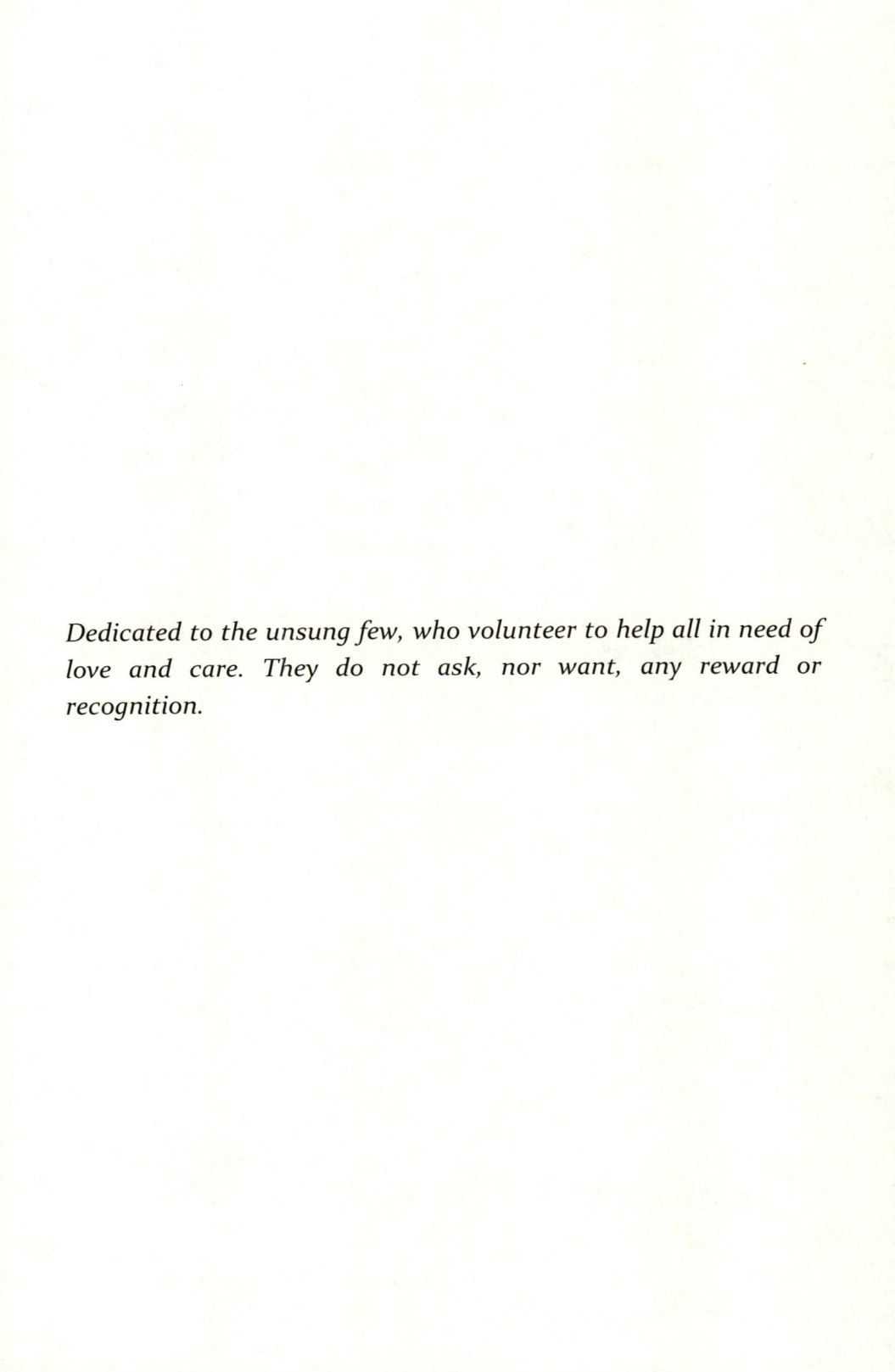

Dedicated to the unsung few, who volunteer to help all in need of love and care. They do not ask, nor want, any reward or recognition.

Table of Contents

The Silence of the Starlings 1
Milestones 7
The Bystander 10
The Lady in Red 15
For the Sins of his Father 23
Embrace of the Tooth Fairies 30
Moonlight Serenade 32
The Spice Girls 39
Dead Certain 44
Three Kings and a Joker 50
A Brief History of Mine 58
Not the Final Frontier 64
Stones with Stories 70
It's Spring Again 73
The Children of Conflict 77
The Last Battle 80
A Good Man 83
The Coral Beneath the Waves 90
The Last of the Red-Hot Losers 97
Award Acceptance Speech 100
Dying to Clothe You 103
Perhaps You have Lost Your Vision 107
Swing Me Just a Little Bit Higher 111
A Case for Compassion 116
Three Blind Mice 119

Paul's Roast 122
Where is the Eagle? 125
A Cloud on Our Horizon 132
A Minute in the Life of Napoleon 134
Heroes of the Human Spirit 137
Doug's Roast 141
Where Have All the Leaders Gone? 144
A Mishap at a Hot and Steamy Place 151

The Lady in Red and Other Works

The Silence of the Starlings

March 1, 1954

A blinding flash on the horizon was followed by a deafening roar. The sky turned orange and melded into yellow a few moments later. The sea near the Marshall Islands was no longer tranquil. An ominous sound rumbled across the ocean, pushing whitecaps from the direction of the far-away islands. A dead silence followed.

"What was that? Hopefully not a volcano erupting. The seas will be rough. We had better leave now."

From above, flakes began to fall and the fishermen brushed them off. The radio man let some of the flakes fall on his tongue.

"What are these? Looks like snowflakes."

"Tastes funny." The radio man spat flakes from his tongue onto the deck.

The twenty-three fishermen on the Lucky Dragon 5, headed back to Yaizu, a port on the east coast of Japan, more than two thousand miles away.

After they arrived they began to unload their catch at the dock. Suddenly the radio man collapsed. His crew mates tried to lift him but they too, were nauseous. Others on the boat called out to workers on the dock for help. Sick ones were taken home suffering from what appeared to be exhaustion.

Within five days, Matashichi Oishi, the chief radio officer, was dead. The cause was determined to be acute organ malfunction. The incident was widely reported following the blast. However, Edward Teller, the father of the hydrogen bomb that had been exploded sixty miles away, on Bikini Island, said later: *"It's unreasonable to make such a big deal about the death of a fisherman."*

Rachel put down the newspaper. *How can an eminent scientist talk that way?*

June 1956

On a small farm near Baltimore, Roger picked up a dead starling. "Wonder what happened to her?"

"Could be an illness. Oh no! There's another one behind the tree. It looks like it's still alive." The bird was on its back, shaking violently and then, in a matter of seconds, it lay still.

"What could be doing this? Do you think there is something in the air?" He asked his guardian.

"And in the soil. See. Look at all these earthworms." The boy picked up six lifeless earthworms.

Overhead, a small plane dropped another cloud of pesticide on the field. The fog enveloped them, but they did not look up, since this was a common occurrence in a farming area.

March 1959. Location. A chemical manufacturer's facility in the USA.

"Did you read the story today?"

"Yes, I did. We don't look very good. Too many people believe her and that spells trouble. A hysterical woman who is fanning the flames that will burn us."

"You need to do something about her. She can't continue like this. She's a Commie. No doubt about it. There's far too much damage being done to us by this woman. I believe she's about to speak to a lot of people who are very important to us. Things could change quickly. You need to stop her. Fast. Pretty damn fast. Do you understand what I mean?"

George nodded. He understood. This had not happened to them before. The woman had to be stopped. He left the office shaking his head. How was it possible that she could get away with this? After all his company had done to save so many lives, one person appears on the scene, from nowhere, and gets noticed. A mere woman, doing so much damage to the company's reputation.

He picked up the phone and called his contact in the news organization that favoured his industry.

"She's at it again. Can you run a story on her? We'll give you some background and some people to interview. She's a raving lunatic, full of BS but is getting a lot of attention and positive comments, which she doesn't deserve."

George gave more details to his contact. "Ok, see you this evening. Same place?"

The following day there was a televised report. The interviewer asked his guest: "How can America listen to a spinster who appears to show concern for the future of our children? She has very little experience and has been scorned by many scientists, one of whom is with us today." He turned to his guest. "Professor Schaefer, tell us what you know about this wonder product that has saved so many lives and is now being criticized by this woman."

"Thank you for inviting me today. We really need to set the record straight here. During the war, we saved thousands of our troops by using DDT. Not only our troops, but the populations in the countries we liberated. They were dying by the thousands until this product was used. There has been no other product I know of, in my lifetime, that has done so much good, for so many people as this wonder chemical. I, as a scientist, am astounded that there are some people who have not embraced the great strides we have made in our field. I have worked in the industry for many years and am proud of the contribution we have made to the betterment of lives here in America and around the world. That is why I am so disturbed that there are some who actually believe the nonsense that is being written by this woman."

"So, tell me Professor, is this woman a liar?"

"I don't think that she is one. But I feel that she strongly believes she is right and we know that she isn't. We have the facts. It disturbs us, as scientists, when people come along with findings that have little, or no basis, in science and then scare the population. Instead of calling her a liar I would prefer to say that she is someone who wants to create a sensation. We have similar parallels with women claiming that organic food is the only kind of food to eat; but if it wasn't for the loving care our farmers give to their fruits and vegetables with harmless pesticides, we would likely have a famine in this great nation."

"Similar to what is happening in Russia?"

"Yes, but it could be worse. We cannot stop the clock on progress. We must advance, find better solutions to the problems facing humanity. Our future lies in chemicals. Without them we will have mass starvation. Insecticides and herbicides are needed now more than ever. Economies have suffered because of the war. Agriculture has been destroyed in many parts of Europe and the chemical revolution is the only thing that can save the world."

"Would you say this person is alarming our citizens needlessly by writing and speaking about something she knows very little about? Would you say that she may be more dangerous that Stalin or Hitler?"

"In what way?'

"Well, millions of people could die of malaria and other diseases carried by insects and vermin. If this would happen couldn't she be called a mass murderer?"

"As a person of science, I can only look at the facts. We have proven that DDT is completely safe for humans. We have sprayed thousands of tons in our fields and have virtually eliminated insects that have destroyed our crops. Remember that the man who discovered this beneficial use of DDT was given the Nobel Prize for Chemistry. If such a reputed organization bestows this honour on a scientist, how can one unmarried woman, with insufficient credentials, challenge us scientists?"

"Thank you, Professor. You've convinced me and hopefully, the American people. This woman needs to talk to more to experts in the industry like yourself before making ridiculous claims that ultimately cause significant damage to the industry and to our health."

On April 3, 1963 the fifty-six-year-old woman sat quietly in her chair and addressed the CBS reporter. She had made sure that only a few of her friends knew of her state of health. Rachel did not have much time left. Cancer had spread to other parts of her body but her task was not complete. Her biological clock was quickly running down.

"Do you feel that the criticism against your book is justified? I mean, there is no doubt that DDT has saved millions of lives by eradicating the mosquito. What do you think about Monsanto's article 'The Desolate Year' which is a parody of your book?"

"I am not against pesticides. We must have insect control. I do not favour turning nature over to insects. I favour the sparing, selective and intelligent use of chemicals. It is the indiscriminate, blanket spraying that I oppose."

Against considerable odds, and in the face of vicious opposition by industry, she left a lasting legacy. The author of *Silent Spring*, died in her home in Maryland. Roger remembers his guardian and grand aunt, Rachel Carson, who died on April 14, 1964. He remembers her more fondly when he walks in the meadows in early April and listens to the chorus of starlings and sparrows.

The dead of winter need not be followed by a silent spring.

Milestones

The police officer stood a little bit farther from the airport vendor selling aromatic *sheesh kebabs*. I would likely never savour these again. This was the same officer who had reviewed my passport application and stated that there were errors in it. *Why was he here? On the day that I was departing the country?* I pretended I hadn't seen him as we approached the departure gate. I didn't dare look back to see if he was coming towards us. We boarded the aircraft but I was still uneasy. I watched each passenger that followed us, certain that the policeman would enter the aircraft and take us off the plane to pay any 'fees' due to him. But the door closed and the SAS Boeing 727 taxied down the runway. In a few minutes, we were aloft and on our way. My tension abated and I began to breathe normally again. My mother smiled at me and squeezed my hand. She was as relieved as I was, that we were finally leaving a country where we had perhaps overstayed our welcome.

The lights faded into the choking smog of that overcrowded city. There were friends that I had left behind. Colleagues that I would never see again. Teachers who had been kind to me during the years that I had attended St. Patrick's High School. Priests who had guided me when I was in that magnificent cathedral that still stands today, behind a white marble monument that glistens and sparkles in the moonlight under threatening clouds. This was no longer a pleasant home. The seeds of intolerance were taking root.

We were on the way to a world I had been made aware of through Johnny Horton's song *'Whispering Pines'*. There was also the movie *'The Trap'*, with Oliver Reed, which featured forests of tall trees, rushing mountain rivers and crisp mountain air. That land was to be our destination. And then there would be snow. Something I had never seen, or felt, before. Snowflakes which would kiss my face a thousand times. We were to join my brother, Bert, who was the pioneer in the family. His many letters to us showed that he had been smitten by the country and the kindly people in his new-found home.

We landed in Montreal. I saw, for the first time, two blonde ground stewardesses. They kidded each other as they checked our papers.

"Finished?"

"No, I'm Canadian," the other replied.

The first joke I heard on Canadian soil. I was exhilarated that I was in a country where I could feel safe. A few hours later we were aloft again and on the final leg of our long journey. Mum was asleep already and likely dreaming of reuniting with her eldest son. Shortly thereafter, I fell into a deep slumber, after having been awake and excited on the longest trip of my life, on a real jet.

The captain's announcement awoke me when we began our descent. I saw jagged mountains and a river meandering like a ribbon of silver in the twilight. We disembarked at McCall Field, now the Calgary International Airport. Weary travellers welcomed to a land of promise. The city had three hundred and sixty thousand people at that time, considerably less than the city of millions which we had left.

The new land did indeed fulfil my dreams. I marvelled at white-capped mountains while I stood by rivers as these rumbled through the valleys. I was awe-struck, standing below the large spruce trees reaching up to dazzling blue skies. I shivered in the cold, clear waters off coastal beaches. This was not a dream. It was real!

For me, a major event in my life was stepping onto Canadian soil. In life, it is the milestones that are celebrated. These have special significance every decade, and every century. Each decade that I have aged, has been filled with happenings that are etched in my memory. There were years when I lost those that I loved. But then, there were times when new loved ones entered by life to accompany me on the road where others had walked before, planting their own memories along the path. It was a year after Canada's centennial celebration that I had landed in Canada. Now I was celebrating a milestone birthday of my own, while Canada turned one hundred and fifty. Happy Birthday to Canada, and to me.

The snowflakes fall, as winter calls, and time just seems to fly. The lyrics tug at my heartstrings as I think of that time, so long ago, when I landed in my forever home.

The Bystander

I saw her being killed. And I did nothing.

Words can be powerful. Words can tug at your heartstrings. And words can kill. But that was the choice she had made. And it was words that had killed her. I wish I could have acted faster.

My name is Meg. That's all you need to know. I didn't like politicians. Well, most of them anyway. They promise whatever you want, but, once elected, they bend in whatever direction the wind blows. They call it 'flexibility`. Listening to their constituents. I call it 'lying'. Breaking promises. Shattering dreams. All, while feeding like gluttons from the public trough.

But then I met this woman. It was at a debate with three other candidates. She was young. Must have been around thirty. Maybe even in her late twenties. I wondered why such a small, attractive person with good manners would enter into the political arena to participate in character assassination, mud-slinging and trash talk.

She conducted herself well in the debate. Surprisingly well, considering she was new to this rough and tumble game and on the same stage as seasoned liars and scumbags of the political world. That evening I spoke to her. After the usual pleasantries, I asked: "What's a nice woman like you doing in a business like this? You're not the type for this job. You appear to be too kind and gentle for this game."

"I will love it," she smiled. "I want to make a change."

I nodded amiably. I had heard that countless times. "That is what all politicians say. Do you really think you can shake up the Establishment? In this country? At this time? And what about late-night phone calls, abusive emails and death threats once you get elected?"

"There will always be risks. It doesn't matter. There are issues I want to fight for. Are you not appalled by how the rich get richer in our country while some of my constituents survive on a meagre pension after working for fifty years? Do you think it is fair that what our Finance Minister spends on dinner can feed an old couple for a week? And why our Prime Minister continues to allow sale of weapons to countries which terrorize their own people with those same weapons?"

Just then another person interrupted. "It's time to leave, Love. The kids are waiting." He turned to me, "I'm sorry."

She smiled and shook my hand. "You will see. I hope I can count on your vote."

A healthy democracy needs young people with energy and new ideas. A nation cannot stagnate in the ways of yesteryear. At this time there are thugs in power in some countries. Their tentacles reach across oceans to our own shores and they commit murder under our noses. We need strong leadership now to deal with rogue nations. But are young people like her, the right type to protect us and run our country?

My husband and I spoke about corrupt and dangerous leaders that evening.

"They are bastards! The lowest of the low, yet they get elected by gullible people," he muttered. "But we need more tough guys in our government. The woman today is too naïve. And she has so little experience. She won't get very far."

"Yes, but that is how all politicians start out. We should vote for her. Don't you think? Maybe we need some idealistic young people to shake up that institution we call our government. All they do is look after themselves. Some have served many years, and you still see empty seats in Parliament since they are likely gadding about town instead of helping to run the country. Where are our representatives? Schmoozing with the elite? We need someone like her."

"She won't get my vote."

"Why not?" I asked him.

"She will never make any headway. There is an old Boys Club that runs this country. They are into everything. Besides, her opponents have powerful friends. She doesn't have friends like that, and never will. It will be a wasted vote."

"It won't be, Eric." I said. "Wherever in the world you look you will see old goats who have been in power for too many years. After the second term, the rot sets in. Look at Robert Mugabe. Our Prime Minister and many other world leaders expected him to make positive changes. He was very popular and had very good intentions when he first took power in the seventies. Now he is in his nineties, still hanging onto power while the whole country has collapsed around him in the last forty years. It's true what they say: 'Power corrupts and absolute power corrupts absolutely'. Maybe we should set limits of two terms for our Prime Minister. That's the only good thing about the American political system."

Eric picked up the newspaper again and muttered. "You're dreaming, Meg."

Some weeks later I was pleasantly surprised to see that she had been elected. I had voted for her. Eric had done so too, with a little nudging. A few months later I saw her rise through the ranks. Maybe, I thought, she <u>would</u> change the world.

It was a bright June afternoon. I hummed a tune to myself as I walked to the train station and passed the library. 'Meet your parliamentarian today' was the sign outside the door. Our elected officials would occasionally have one-on-one talks with their constituents in this library.

Then I saw her. She was leaving the building with another man. He was much older. Possibly in his seventies. They were stopped by a man in a rumpled raincoat. She smiled at me as I passed by and turned to the man who wanted to speak to her. Then I heard voices being raised. And three loud bangs. Firecrackers at this time of the day?! But then someone screamed. The man in the raincoat had pulled out a knife. Its blade glistened in the strong sunlight as he raised it above him and then thrust it down several times. She fell to the pavement. The old man fell on his knees clutching his stomach and groaning. I watched, unable to move. A dumb bystander. Finally, I rushed towards her as others did too. Someone chased the man into an alleyway. Another was trying to staunch the blood pouring out of her as she lay on the pavement. A lady was on her cellphone calling Emergency.

On June 16, 2016, Jo Cox was killed by a man who was galvanized into action by the rhetoric of politicians in the debate for, and against, Britain's membership in the European Union. Jo had briefly lit our small world with her enthusiasm but was the victim of an act of hate. I wish I could have changed her mind when I had first met her.

In my remaining life there is so much more to do. Helping others. Children of conflict. Victims of hunger. Old, lonely people looking out the windows of their homes waiting for someone to visit them. Jo had spoken for them. But powerful rhetoric and divisive words had led to her murder.

I'm a fifty-year-old woman. I'm going to do something about it. I will run in the next election. Pick up the work that Jo had started.

The Lady in Red

The eastbound subway hissed, slowed and stopped at the platform. Commuters stood shoulder to shoulder but made space for those disembarking. Dan watched as the passengers boarded. The last person to enter the train, turned, looked at him and dropped her purse on the platform shortly before the doors closed. It was too late for him to return it. He had noticed that she had red hair under the hood of her red coat. But that was all he could see. He put the purse into his pocket.

On returning home, after eating his supper he opened the purse. It was small, with a fifty dollar note and some coins. A piece of paper that had been torn out of a notebook showed only part of a Boston address and an apartment number 505.

The following week he saw a woman with a red coat on the same platform. He walked over but then noticed that she was less tall and did not have red hair.

A month later he entered a McDonalds Restaurant for a quick snack. When he got up to leave, someone tapped his shoulder. He turned around. It was one of the staff.

"This is for you, sir." His name was on a manila envelope.

"How do you know me? I've never seen you before."

"I don't. There was a lady who left after you arrived and she asked me to give this to you. She said she was in a hurry and would see you later if you can find her. I assumed she was a friend of yours and wanted to play Hide-and-Seek or something."

"What did she look like?"

"She had sunglasses and was wearing a red coat. Tall and slim. Very attractive if I may say so."

"Did she have red hair?"

"Yes. She seems to be a very nice person and left me a sizeable tip to give this to you."

Dan opened the envelope. There was a printed message. 'My first name begins with an 'E'. You are somebody that I will never forget.' *This woman was playing games with him. She must have deliberately dropped that purse on the platform. He was being stalked. But why?*

That evening Dan did not watch the *Boston Bruins* in the NHL playoffs. He was too preoccupied by this woman who was leading him on. Who was she, and why was she doing this? There were only three women he had worked with, or who were friends, with a first name beginning with an 'E'. Esther was one of his colleagues at work. Elizabeth was the wife of his friend, Brent, and Estelle was a former girl-friend. His three previous wives were Melissa, Norma and Jane. None of them had red hair and neither would they play games with him. None of them would ever write 'I will never forget you'. They had no reason to do that.

A month later an envelope arrived in his mailbox. There was no return address but there was a faint smell of perfume on a piece of torn, black lace. 'Do you remember me now?' Dan examined the piece of lace under a lamp. It may have been cut from a woman's panties. In recent months he had dated at least six women. They had parted company and he did not recall any who wore black lace. He looked inside the envelope again and found the inner flap had the complete address 'Apt 505, 666 Appleby Street'. He looked at an online map and found a street named Appleby on the other side of Boston.

Dan was beginning to enjoy this 'treasure hunt'. She was definitely a person of great value. For a few nights at least. He had never been stalked by someone before. His heart raced and his penis rose in anticipation of the upcoming tryst.

The following Friday he found the apartment building. He took the elevator to the fifth floor. Apartment 505 was around the corner. Dan knocked on the door. He smelled the roses in the bouquet he had purchased. Soft and delicate. Hopefully there would be in a passionate embrace soon after he presented them to her.

"Just a minute. Be right there." A woman's voice answered.

A few moments later the door opened. It was the redhead in form-fitting black tights. He recognized the perfume from the envelope. Dan's hormones were now in overdrive. "You finally found me," she said.

"Thank goodness. Here's your purse. I have enough money."

"Thank you. Come in. Take a seat. We have lots to talk about."

She guided him to a sofa and then placed the roses in the kitchen sink. Across from him was a large painting of a falcon sitting atop a barbed wire fence. In its beak was a small animal, perhaps a field mouse. There were no other pictures on the walls. A black wine bottle held three white lilies on the coffee table in between the two couches.

"But how did you know my name? Where did we meet? I don't recognize you."

"Would you like a glass of wine?"

"Certainly. If it's red."

"That's all us redheads drink. Didn't you know that?" She winked and stalked into the kitchen in her stockinged feet as he treated himself to the view of her perfect ass. "I already have one opened so that it gets some air. It's got good body too."

Dan was tempted to say 'Just like yours'. But instead asked: "Is it a Merlot?"

"Nicer than that. It is similar to Chateau Mouton Rothschild which I was introduced to many years ago when I was dating a wine connoisseur. A little bit less expensive though."

She gave him the glass and settled onto the couch on the other side of the coffee table. "So, what have you been doing with yourself all these years? We have so much to talk about." She tilted her head and crossed her legs. He couldn't wait to roll down those tights and enjoy the feel of her naked skin against his.

She was leading the conversation. It was like he was being interviewed. By a prospective boss. He was an alpha male and was unaccustomed to this role change. She smiled and sipped her wine. He took a gulp of his and was already feeling the buzz. "Nice wine indeed."

"I asked 'what have you been doing all these years'?"

"Well I have been married and divorced three times in the last thirty years. Just didn't work out. It was me really. I guess I was too controlling. Occupational hazard for a cop, I guess. Come home and can't shake the habit." He laughed.

"Your wives. What were they like?"

"Pretty and cute. Perhaps a bit too cute."

"No. I meant, their temperament? Intimidated by you since you were a cop? Did you beat them up?"

Dan shifted on the couch. This woman seemed to be provoking him. He felt that perhaps he should play this strange game as long as they ended up in the bedroom really quick. "Why are you asking me this? You don't know me. I'm not that kind of a person. Maybe a little rough play in bed but that was all. The women liked it." Dan studied her more closely. "I feel that I have met you before. Not sure where, though. Or perhaps I just saw you on the subway a couple of times."

"We met once. It was a long time ago. An unforgettable experience." She rose, went to the kitchen and brought the wine bottle, refilled his glass and left it on the coffee table. She sat opposite him again. He yearned to grab her and kiss her hard on the mouth and smear that crimson lipstick all over her face and neck. She was a knockout.

He hadn't realized that he had gulped down his first glass already. "Thank you." He said, as he took a sip. "This tastes a bit different."

"It is. Swirl it around in your mouth. You'll appreciate it more." She demonstrated with her wine, licking her lips after she took a sip. Dan hoped she would move and sit next to him on the couch. Perhaps she was waiting for the right moment to make a move. Like the falcon whose eyes seemed to be fixed on him.

"Ah. You are right. I'm feeling as if I'm on air right now. That's a really good wine."

"Now tell me, Dan. Why is it you don't remember me when we had met previously? The circumstances were a bit different. Not as pleasant. But certainly, something I could never forget. It was quite a night." She paused and raised her glass in a toast. "For you that is."

"I really can't place you. Are you sure it was me?"

"I'm dead certain it was you, Dan. But you, you don't even remember my name. Why is that?" She rose from the sofa and came across to his side. But she did not sit down next to him. She stood above him and held his chin so that he could look directly into her eyes. Now, do you remember?"

"I'm sorry. You didn't even tell me your name." His hand started to tremble.

"You didn't ask when we first met. Why should I tell you now?"

"I don't get it. I still think you are mistaking me for someone else."

"Interesting." She looked at him coolly. "Put your mind back to your days in college. Here in Boston. The campus bar. Mid eighties."

"That was more than thirty years ago. Did we ever date?"

"Well, let's say you had intimate contact with me. After you slipped something into my drink."

Dan tried to lift the glass but was unable to do so. Instead the wine spilled on his lap. "Sorry," he said. But he couldn't move to clean up the mess on his lap, or the sofa. "I must be drunk already."

She sat down next to him and put her hand on his thigh. "No, you are not drunk. The drink will take some time to act. Paralysis is the first stage. Amazing what a pharmacist can cook up. Done a number of experiments which worked well.

Especially on my late husband. The asshole. Piss be upon him." She raised her glass again in a mock toast.

"Why are you doing this? Is this a date rape drug?" Dan still could not move the lower part of his body although he was fully conscious of his surroundings and could feel her hand on his thigh.

"Not exactly. But let me refresh your memory. Or should I say your 'selective memory'. You seem to have forgotten what you did to me. Or perhaps you had raped many other women in college and lost track. For you it was normal, I guess. That's why you don't remember. There may have been too many victims. One just like the other."

She went to the kitchen and brought back a large kitchen knife. Dan tried to struggle but he was totally helpless. She took an apple from a fruit bowl on the counter and sliced it with a quick wrist movement. The knife was sharp. Very sharp.

"It's Swedish steel. The best for cooks. And for cutting meat." She pointed it at his throat. "Tell me, Dan. Don't you remember the incident which started in the bar on the campus? You drugged me and took me to a dark corner on the campus and raped me. Then you took me back to the bar and left me outside the front door so that everyone thought that I was a fucking slut." She cut the front of his shirt with a quick stroke exposing his chest. "It got worse. Two other men did the same to me that night. I had to have an abortion." Another motion with the knife and his fly and underwear were sliced, exposing his now flaccid member. "I will deal with the other two after I have finished with you."

"What do you want to do to me?" asked Dan.

She smiled, walked to the kitchen, picked up the phone and dialled a number. Dan could hear a man answer. She asked: "Can you come by in an hour? I should be done by then."

For the Sins of his Father

"Good Morning. I'm Dan Griswold and this is the Griswold Report. We have with us today General Robert Clements, who has served with our troops overseas. The General had contacted the station regarding an important message he wanted to deliver to Americans. This morning we will find out what the message is, that is so important to us Americans. Why do you want to talk to us, General?"

"Thank you, Dan, for granting me this interview at such short notice. I hope what I have to say, will help future generations who wish to make our world a better place." The General took a sip from a glass of water. "When I was a young boy I was walking to school with one of the girls in the neighbourhood. She stopped when she saw two boys laughing. One of them had a struggling gopher in his hands. She asked them 'What are you doing?' as the other grabbed its hind legs."

"Excuse me, General, is this a story about animal abuse? We ran one last month."

"No, it's not. Please let me finish."

"Ok. Sorry. Please continue."

"The kids holding the gopher were trying to pull off its legs. The girl said. 'Stop it. You can't do that. You're hurting the animal.' The boys were surprised. 'But we are going to kill it.

It's only a pest.' The girl pulled the gopher out of the boy's hands and set it free. It scurried away. I was startled by her action against the bigger kids."

"But General, what is this leading to? Why did you call us? It must be more important than a couple of kids being mean to gophers."

"What happened years ago has remained with me. I wish I had a conscience like the girl in my neighbourhood. I have been troubled recently by a number of events. Let me rephrase that. Sorry. I have been troubled for many years by what I have been witness to, or heard about, while serving our great nation. And there comes a time when more citizens need to be made aware of the harsh reality of war. For many years, I had a good job. I had enlisted because I wanted to protect my country. But what I saw disturbed me. Deeply. I recently reported my concerns to my superiors and they told me they would take care of it."

"What did they do?"

"Nothing."

"Why was that?"

"Possibly somewhere up the chain of command, or perhaps when it got to Washington, the issue was killed or the paperwork was lost. I should also mention, Dan, that my commanding officer does not know about this interview. I will likely face disciplinary action for this. Possibly labeled as a traitor. I have seen that happen to other whistleblowers."

"Hope you get to keep your job, General. But why do you want to talk directly to our listeners? What is it that troubles you? We have heard all the issues about PTSD, insufficient aid to veterans, lack of jobs for returning veterans and so on. What is so different about your story? You mentioned to me that it is a very urgent matter."

"I feel that we, as officers, must maintain the highest conduct of personal and ethical behaviour. To the best of my knowledge, those who served under me followed my example. However, there were others in leadership positions who need to be guided back to the right path. Their subordinates were committing crimes which were not reported. Or had they been, they were not handled by a military court. I had talked to some of the officers myself but they told me that it was not my business to interfere with how they ran their units."

"Are there not codes of conduct that we adhere to in the Forces?"

"Only on paper, for some. Sadly. It is very difficult to know what is going on in the field. Men are taught to be aggressive. Taught to fight. Taught to win at any costs. Such is the nature of war. Be mean. Be nasty. Intimidate the enemy. Get your revenge."

"So, after you reported the concerns, whatever they were, to your commanding officer and got no response, what did you do to pursue the matter further?"

"I wrote a letter to my Commanding Officer with a copy to the Chief of Staff. It detailed the event that took place in the field and asked that a review be done of the case. This was one of possibly other such events. I will relate to you what I know." The General took another gulp of water. "The troops were under the command of a Colonel in another unit who was working closely with the CIA on the ground. Our troops had located a house that likely harboured the enemy. Our planes dropped four, five-hundred-pound bombs on the roughly hundred by one-hundred-and-fifty-foot square compound.

The building was pounded for four hours by our forces. It was not likely that there were any survivors. Several rounds were also fired, before, and after, the bombing. One of our men was killed, another wounded. However, when our Special Forces looked through the rubble they found someone who was still alive. He was then shot twice, in the back, at close range. He did not die. He was taken to a military hospital and kept there for interrogation by the CIA."

"General, how did you get this information? Also, this seems to be normal in warfare. People get killed. Die. Brutally. Sometimes the enemy is put out of their misery. Isn't that good?"

"It was from one of my own soldiers who had been told about it by one of the troops at the compound on that day. It was disturbing that one of our men would shoot a wounded enemy in the back. Worse still was what was done to him at the base. That is not military conduct and is certainly not normal in warfare."

"Did the soldier not report it to his own commander?"

"I don't believe so. Maybe this was routine. Or maybe he had reported previous incidents and these were brushed off. After all, these guys were all terrorists. The soldier who shot him in the back was never held accountable. Later I had heard that there was a confidential report prepared for the Department of Defense that concluded that the field report was 'doctored'. There was a possibility that our soldier was killed by friendly fire. One survivor was possibly executed on the spot, and the other kept alive for interrogation. The doctor who had examined the survivor stated that there were two large exit wounds and that he was missing the upper part of his chest. There was also another issue."

"What was that?"

"The person taken prisoner was a boy. A child soldier. This is totally against our own ethics and the UN Protocol regarding rights of a child in war zones. Furthermore, the boy was tortured by our own people. We have lost all reason when it comes to the treatment of someone who is labelled a terrorist. Which takes me back to the struggling gopher. He was a pest. So, torturing and killing the pest, or the terrorist, is perfectly acceptable. We choose the word 'terrorist' very conveniently to dispatch our perceived enemies. Terrorists are now scapegoats who can be tortured with impunity. Scapegoats have existed in some cultures for centuries and still do. One such religion anoints a goat that is set free in the desert to die of thirst and starvation. A sacrifice to atone for the sins of their own community. In former times, mentally or physically ill people were driven out of the community or beaten, hanged or drowned to offer them as a sacrifice to save our own souls."

"So, where did we go wrong? How did it get to this, General?"

"I believe it began many years ago with the Western world turning a blind eye to the human rights abuses in the Middle East and other countries. We used the same 'terrorists' to help us get rid of the Russians in Afghanistan. Now they have turned against us. Also, cheap oil was very important to us. The West pandered to these countries because of cheap oil. The wealthy nations in the Middle East are brainwashing children in their country and many other countries. Theirs is a cruel and inhumane doctrine from the Middle Ages. Beheadings take place every Friday, after prayers, in what is called Chop-Chop Square in Riyadh. No westerners are allowed there. Many of the beheadings are performed on women and girls. These women, girls or men, are workers from poor countries like India, Bangladesh, Pakistan, Egypt and the Philippines. We have known about this for years, and have never made a serious attempt to stop the abhorrent treatment of persons in these wealthy nations in the Middle East. I do not see this ending soon. We have a generation of young men whose sole purpose is to kill infidels, wherever they may be. But we continue to support the regimes in the Middle East who finance terrorism and warp the minds of so many young children there. They will all become child soldiers."

"What can be done now, General?"

"We do not have the right leadership now in the US to begin to solve this problem. I see a bleak future for my children and grand-children. If any action is taken now, it will take at least three generations before we are successful. But we must start to take action now. It is important for us Americans to regain our conscience. I joined the Military because I was once a man of honour. I may have lost my conscience along the way. I must pay the price for what I didn't succeed with, more than a decade ago."

"We are running out of air time now. Thank you, General, for sharing your views with us. But tell me, who was the young prisoner?"

"I was never given his name. Perhaps you can find out. I am running out of time too. I was at my grandson's fourteenth birthday yesterday. That's how young this boy was. Just a young, misguided boy. Why should he have had to pay for the sins of his father?"

The General left the studio. Shortly thereafter, the sound of a single gunshot was heard from the lobby of the television station.

Embrace of the Tooth Fairies

"Can you tell me a story, Grandpa?"

"OK, but instead of telling me stories, my dad used to buy me comic books. In those days Archie comics were my favourite."

"Archie?"

"You've never heard of Archie and Veronica?"

"Nope. Was Veronica his wife?"

"No. His girl-friend. Although Betty liked him too."

"Did you have lots of girl-friends when you were young, Grandpa?"

"No. Only one. Your grandma. She was a real cutie-pie and whenever I saw her in school she would smile at me but I was too shy to talk to her. With my big ears and buckteeth, all the kids used to make fun of me, so I kept to myself."

"But you don't have buckteeth, Grandpa."

"I used to, Jimmy. Not anymore. As they say, 'my teeth are like the stars. They come out at night'. But, as I was saying, I really took a fancy to Grandma. So one day I wrote her a Christmas card, asked my dad for a penny and mailed it to her house."

"Did she send you back a Christmas card?"

"No. But when we were alone in the schoolyard after the holidays, I finally screwed up the courage to ask her if she got my card. She said 'I did get a card from you but my name is not Veronica.' 'I'm so sorry', I said. Then she leaned over and kissed me."

"Wow, that must have been nice."

"Well, in a way."

"What do you mean? Didn't you want her to kiss you? Wasn't that your dream?"

"Yeah, but she was wearing braces and so was I. We couldn't disengage the braces. We were stuck. So we went to Father O'Grady, our principal. He looked at us and shook his head. He brought a tub of water and dunked our heads into it. We were free! But then I said 'But Father, isn't it said that 'what God hath joined together, let no man put asunder'. You put us under! He smiled at my joke and said 'I will marry you when the time comes'. And that is why Grandma and Grandpa got married."

Moonlight Serenade

Bertie bundled himself in his blanket and hoped to warm his skinny body while the temperature outside hovered at forty degrees Fahrenheit, an unusually cold night for Agra. He liked to sleep with the windows open since he preferred the coolness of the night, and also loved to awaken to the cooing of the pigeons which nested in the tamarind tree in the garden. He would often throw cooked rice on the ground beneath the tree for them to eat in the mornings, before the chickens woke up and ate the rest. He loved birds and spent more time with pigeons, parrots, chickens and ducks than with his siblings or friends.

As he dozed off he wondered if it would get even colder on Christmas Eve, which was only a week away. Sleep came easily to him since he had spent the evening dancing with his imaginary girlfriend to *Moonlight Serenade*, his all time favourite record. Bertie was a dreamer, quite unlike his younger brother and older sister who were more extroverted and often tried to get him involved in rough and tumble games, but to no avail. He, and they, accepted that he was a dreamer and would remain that way for all of his life. But the dreamer had a dream that night that he would remember for many years.

Deep in slumber he dreamt that he was on a tarmac next to a plane with high wings. It was unlike the Spitfire model aircraft he had seen which Herman had built. It was cold, very cold, while he shivered in his cotton pyjamas. Since he had never stood next to a real airplane before, he ran his hand on the fuselage which was smooth and curved, with little rivets every two feet. He knocked on the metal and was surprised by the hollow sound. The fuselage was thin and tight, somewhat similar to the skin on a drum, which he had recently received for his tenth birthday. *How odd*, he thought.

The airfield was shrouded in a heavy fog quite unlike the mists he had experienced in Mandalay, or Agra. His sensitive nostrils picked up an overpowering smell of fuel, as if he was standing close to a petrol station. *Perhaps the airplane's tank had recently been filled and some fuel may have dropped on the tarmac.* He looked down but could not see in the gloom. His feet were not wet so he assumed he was not standing in a puddle of petrol. Bertie shivered and peered through the fog while holding his nose to keep out the smell of petrol. *It would surely would damage his delicate lungs.* He was careful about his health and would always dress warmly, use a handkerchief to blow his nose so as not to spread germs, wash his hands frequently and brush his teeth for at least fifteen minutes every day. *But why didn't he have his coat? He could catch pneumonia with this terrible chill in the air!*

A slight breeze shifted the cloud of fog and he saw three men in uniform walked towards the airplane. They were tall. Much taller than his father. He could hear their voices as they approached.

"It's after noon and we are late," said a voice.

"Good afternoon, sirs," he said, but they didn't hear him.

"Are you sure we should be flying on a day like this?" A man asked.

"It's always like this in December. Miserable fog, every day and every night but we keep flying," his companion answered. Two men entered the plane while the third walked towards the nose of the aircraft ready to turn the propeller.

"Where the hell are the parachutes?" One of the men inside the plane asked. Bert could see his own reflection in the rimless glasses but he could not see the rest of the man's face in the dense fog.

"What's the matter with you, Miller? Do you want to live forever?"

The man called Miller had a familiar voice but Bertie didn't know anyone called Miller. He knew Mervyn and Melvin, friends of his parents, but nobody by the name of 'Miller'. He followed the two men onto the aircraft and wanted to participate in this great adventure. They were oblivious of his presence. He tried to step in front of them to see their faces but no matter how hard he tried, he just couldn't move his feet to face the two passengers. The pilot rotated the propeller to start the engine, which hammered and hesitated but finally fired on all cylinders. Bertie had never been in a plane before and was thrilled to see the instrument panel light up and cast an eerie glow in the freezing cabin. The pounding of the engine rattled every bone in his body and he held firmly to the back of the seat of the man called Miller. He tried again to move forward to see the faces of the two men in the dim cockpit lights. However, his feet still seemed to be riveted to the floor of the aircraft.

The pilot strapped on his flying harness and settled himself into his seat with his hand on the joystick. The plane started to move. It picked up speed and the rattle of the engine shook the entire machine. Bertie felt himself being pulled to the back of the aircraft. He grabbed the back of the seat to remain standing as they became airborne. *What a thrill! A ten-year-old boy on his first flight with three airmen!* He couldn't wait to tell his brother and sister about this adventure. Bertie's ears stopped popping after the plane had reached cruising altitude. With the engine noise reduced, the conversation between the three men could be heard.

"Won't take us that long to be in Paris with this plane, Colonel. It doesn't have great speed but is built tough. It's a great little plane built in Canada. I flew them while I was in training in Manitoba. Was there for two years. Bloody cold and windy in that part of the world!"

"If it could fly in that bloody cold Canadian winter it should be fine in this fog," said the Colonel. "I don't know why my friend is so nervous."

"I'm not nervous. I just need a drink. Only had three for breakfast."

Miller took a long pull on his cigarette and blew the smoke toward the back of the cabin towards Bertie, whose throat constricted by this unwelcome blue cloud. Twenty minutes after being airborne they were clear of the fog. Below the airplane Bertie gazed intently at the gray water below. *"Where are we?"* He asked himself. Behind him he could see the retreating coastline as the plane banked slightly and then levelled off as the land disappeared in the distance.

"Comfortable back there?" The pilot asked.

"Any booze on the plane?"

"No sir. I was told you may object."

"Me? Object? What a joke! I find it objectionable that there is no booze on the plane for our guest."

A rumbling sound, like rising thunder, could now been heard in the distance, getting closer and closer. What seemed like hundreds of large aircraft were now directly overhead with engines pounding with a deafening drumbeat.

"Look. We've got company above. See those dark shapes? They are Lancasters. Beautiful birds. Must be our boys coming back from a bombing run on the Krauts," the pilot shouted.

Bertie was terrified. He didn't consider those monstrous machines as 'beautiful birds'. Not the birds that he loved in his garden in Agra. Instead he felt that they were Angels of Death. Dark, black, menacing machines with a low rumble that were portendors of death and destruction. *How could the pilot call them beautiful birds?* Bertie wanted to get off the plane. Fast. Very fast. But his feet remained rooted to the floor. His body shook with fear as these dark monsters hovered overhead and cast black shadows on the sea below. A hundred shadows which had likely consumed thousands of lives each time they took to the skies. *My God. Is this what war is all about?* He thought. He wanted to be home safe with his mum and dad and he feared he would never see them again. A few moments later the dark gray of the sea turned to white as the incendiary bombs exploded.

"What the hell?" Someone screamed. "They are dumping their load into the Channel."

"Shit! We must be in the South Jettison Area. Hang on! Let me try to manoeuvre us out of this mess!"

Large grey cylinders hurtled down past the small plane with a sound as terrifying as that of hundreds of pigs being slaughtered. Bright flashes of light and the deafening sound of bombs all around continued for several minutes.

"Hang on. We'll be OK."

"*Mummy!*" Screamed Bertie, who started to cry in terror *"Help me!"*

After another bright flash of light and a deafening explosion, Bertie woke up in his bed, cold and shivering. The sound resonated in his ears and pounded the sides of his head. The bright flashes were still in his vision, as he looked around the bedroom. He thought he was bleeding but instead it was sweat streaming down his face and chest. He gasped for air and swung his legs over the bed in an attempt to stand, but he fell back. His heart finally slowed and he walked unsteadily to the bathroom, relieved himself and then wiped the sweat off his face and body with a towel. Never had he had such a realistic dream. *Where had he been?*

At breakfast the next morning Albert turned on the Phillips short wave radio and tuned in to listen to the latest news on BBC. Instead of the news, the station was playing Bertie's favourite song, *Moonlight Serenade*. The dream from the night before still troubled him and he hardly heard the music. Instead he stuffed jam and bread in his mouth and swallowed hot *chai* to warm his stomach on this winter morning.

The radio crackled and the announcer said: "We hope you enjoyed the music you just heard. The BBC has just received news that a pilot and two passengers, one a Lieutenant Colonel and another a Captain in the American Air Force, are presumed dead after a small plane did not arrive in Paris after leaving Bedford, England. The Royal Air Force reports that it was likely brought down by enemy fire while flying over the English Channel. We regret to inform you that the Captain was none other than Glenn Miller, the most popular band leader of our time. Our heartfelt condolences go to Mrs. Miller and his family."

Bertie coughed up his bread and began to cry. Albert knew that Bertie idolized Glenn Miller.

"It's alright, son. Maybe he survived the crash and they haven't found him yet. They said he was 'presumed dead'. He could have jumped out with his parachute." Albert held Bertie's shaking shoulders.

"No, Dad," Bertie cried. "He is dead! They didn't have parachutes on the plane. I know. I was with them, in my dream last night."

There have been several theories about the disappearance of the small plane that carried Glenn Miller on his flight from Bedford, UK to Paris. One of the more credible theories was that the plane may have been hit when the Allies were returning from an aborted bombing mission in Germany. The planes dumped the bombs in a section of the English Channel designated for this. Crew members of one of the squadrons of Lancaster bombers had seen a plane tailspin into the ocean and one of them had made a record of this in his log. Years later he saw the movie The Glenn Miller Story and reported that the plane he saw was likely the one that spiralled into the English Channel in the afternoon of December 15, 1944.

The Spice Girls

He was sure he would snap. Again. But he rang the bell anyway. "There was a phone call from this home. Someone asked for help."

"Yes, please come in."

Gordon entered the home and was taken to the kitchen. Two women stood next to the man who had let him in. The women were holding each other, cheeks wet with tears. Their faces were pale, with a greenish pallor. The man was silent, eyes downcast.

Before him was a shape. Disfigured beyond recognition. Next to it was a meat cleaver, still dripping. Bones. Lots of them. A large pot was oozing green slime. The putrid odour overpowered him and he wanted to retch. But after so many years in the business, Gordon knew how to control his bodily reaction to what he saw.

He looked at their stained hands with disgust. "Leave the room. I need some space to take photographs."

The three complied and went to the living room where they sat down on the large couch which faced the bay window, looking onto the street where children played, unaware of what had happened in the home. The man sat in the centre and the women on either side. He assumed that the man was the father and that the two younger women were his daughters. Either that, or the old pervert had two saucy young babes. A redhead and a blonde.

He did not recall being on a case like this in the last twenty years of his career. Gordon thought that he had seen it all. Until today.

He put on his gloves and began the inspection. It had been a violent end. Cupboards left with doors open, pots and pans strewn about and kitchen towels smudged red as the perpetrators had quickly tried to cover up their crime. Gordon unpacked his Nikon camera from the kit bag and snapped from various angles. Grimly he entered the living room.

"Where's your computer?"

"Upstairs," the man answered, eyes downcast. "But be careful when you open the brown door."

"It's not brown. It's cinnamon. I painted it myself," the redhead corrected.

"This is not the time to discuss the colour of the door, young lady. The man has a job to do and he may consider it brown, just like I did."

"But…"

"No buts! Please be quiet and show some respect for your elders."

Gordon was no stranger to strained relationships. "What is behind the brown, I mean cinnamon coloured door, that I should be careful about?"

The blonde was about to speak but the man glared at her. She quickly closed her mouth. The two ladies exchanged fearful glances. "There may be a real mess behind the door, that's all. You know how it is with two women in the house. Stuff thrown on the floor. A tripping hazard. I almost broke my nose once when my slippers got caught in a bra thrown on the floor." It was the ladies' turn to glare at the man.

Gordon checked the two rooms upstairs which had their doors open. One appeared to be a den with a computer and two over-stuffed bookshelves. The other was a bedroom, with the bed neatly made up. In the attached bathroom, a razor, toothbrush and toothpaste lay by the sink. He examined the razor. He could see a few hairs still clinging to the blade. *Dirty*, he thought. He always cleaned his own razor after he shaved. *And here the man was complaining about the messy habits of the two women.*

The files on the hard drive of the computer would provide him valuable information. Search history often provided clues. Gordon moved the mouse. The screen awoke from its sleep cycle and showed a website. Bloodied flesh and bones strewn on leaves was shown. Bile roiled up his gullet. He turned away in disgust.

The brown/cinnamon door was at the end of the hallway. Maybe there was another computer in the home. The man had cautioned him about what was behind the door. There could be another gruesome sight to shock him. On the plank floor were several pairs of underwear, jeans and tops. He did not see any bras. Perhaps the warning the man had given to the girls had worked. Two *Ikea* beds with rumpled lavender sheets and quilts were against each of the walls. These had not been made up like in the man's bedroom. Neat-freak Felix Unger, in the *Odd Couple* movie, came to his mind. Although, instead of Oscar the slob, the man had two messy 'slobettes' sharing the home. He was glad he didn't have any children. Gordon's own home was always neat and tidy.

In the women's bathroom all he found was lipstick, tubes of makeup, perfume bottles and several hairbrushes. Nothing out of the ordinary for a couple of women. Gordon closed the bathroom door. The smell of some perfumes made him nauseous. *They must have had a few gallons of those.*

He went downstairs. The three had been whispering to each other but stopped as soon as he came in. Their faces had got back some of their natural colour but were still taut and drawn.

"Ok, who did it?"

The three were silent. The girls' lips trembled but they wouldn't utter a word. The man stared at his hands. Gordon reached into his pocket and removed his note book.

"There was nothing upstairs. But what is in the kitchen is unbelievable. I could take serious action against all three of you who are complicit in this crime. You are stupid, ignorant brutes who do not belong on this earth."

The three looked at the floor and shifted on the couch. The women wanted to escape from the room or to scream in anguish.

Gordon continued: "Capital punishment is too good for you. You should be grilled in Hell for what you have done. You nincompoops should know when to use a knife. You don't use a cleaver on a tomato. And you don't boil lettuce and fenugreek with soup bones!".

He glared at the perpetrators of the heinous crime. "Basil, Rosemary and Ginger, you are a disgrace to the human race. What you did to that cute tomato in the kitchen was horrendous. And your attempt at making soup was beyond belief. Make no bones about it. If I was on my regular beet I could have given you thyme! You are forever banished from the kitchen. If you are ever in there again, you will wish you were never alive..."

Gordon Ramsay closed his case book. Gingerly. He had known something was amiss when he had cumin. Hal LaPino, his assistant, had taken the phone call from this family. He had given him sage advice. Hal was worth his celery.

The celebrity chef slammed the door as he left the house.

Dead Certain

It was already past seven o'clock and she had not noticed the time go by. Neither had she noticed that she was the only one left in the office at that hour.

"Judy, can you bring me the quarterly financials?"

She knew what he wanted. It was not the report. It was always the same. But she needed this job. Badly. That lecherous bastard probably knew that she wouldn't say 'no'. She wasn't the only one he took advantage of. There were a couple of others. Each of them knew, but never discussed it. They couldn't. It was a man's world.

She arranged her hair. *Why had she just done that, dammit? To look more attractive to that man? What was she thinking?* As she walked down the corridor to the corner office she promised herself that this would be the last time. But that's what she had said to herself before. She wondered if his wife knew. Poor woman. Must be hell living with an asshole like him.

Framed photographs of the boss accepting awards for philanthropy in the city had been placed on the walls of the hallway leading to his office. Him with the Mayor. Both smiling like sharks. And there he was with the CEO of the United Way, compassion and caring in his eyes while his patronizing hand was placed on the shoulder of a young child in a wheelchair.

One day, others would find out about him. The cheap prick wouldn't spend a cent of his own when there was company money available for donations. There were expenses to contractors who had done renovations to his home which were charged to the company as well as business trips to Hawaii. No one in Accounting dared to question this. He was the owner of the business. He didn't become the owner through hard work but by marrying the previous owner's daughter. Poor man. If only he knew the bastard who had married his daughter was now plundering company funds. *The man made her sick. If only she could find another job.* In the last two years no job offers came close to her current salary. That was why he paid her so well. She was just a whore. His whore. She hoped her husband would never find out. *He was the kindest, sweetest man a woman could have.*

    She opened the door to the Executive Area. His was the largest of the four offices in the area. The others had already left, otherwise he would not have summoned her. She knocked lightly on his door and pushed it open. His office reeked of whiskey mingled with his body odour. An overpowering combination. She closed and locked the door. That was the routine. The boss rose from his chair and beckoned. She was disgusted by the stupid smile while he drooled. He started to unbuckle his belt. *Why didn't he pick on women closer to his age?* She let her clothing drop to the floor. He walked around the desk, ogling at her nakedness, stroking her skin and brushing her hair back from her face. The old goat panted and wheezed while he rubbed himself against her. His bony fingers groped at the curves and valleys of her body.

    On the wall behind his desk, was a framed photograph of him when he was much younger, with his wife and a child.

A cute little boy. His wife's eyes appeared to be looking at her in dismay. She looked away from the picture as her husband pawed and fondled her, his saliva drooling onto her shoulder, sniffing her skin like a predator, which he was. She could feel his old bones shudder with joy. Judy looked at the clock. Ten minutes. That's all he took. Always. But those ten minutes sucked at her moral core. *How long could she allow this to continue?*

She dressed, smoothed her clothes and left the office and the Executive Area. Wordlessly. The janitor, vacuuming the hallway, stopped as she passed by and smiled at her. *Was it a smile, or a smug grin*? She hoped that he did not know what had just happened behind those doors. Possibly he already knew and would gossip with the others in the Cleaning staff about the macho office boss in the corner office. Perhaps he would some day prey on his own workers if he ever got into a position of power and control. *Fuck you men, you are all alike!*

He turned the corner. The mansion was the third from the left. It was set back farther on the estate protected by a high wall. Brian was familiar with this house. Very familiar. The large trees and dense bushes hid most of the home from the street. Being hidden from public view was so important to residents of this neighbourhood. Ill-gotten treasures were likely locked in the bowels of these homes. An owl hooted as he approached. Brian heard a small animal scurrying through the bushes. The occupant would not be expecting him. He could see a light in the upstairs room and the Mercedes parked on the driveway, instead of in the garage. Perhaps the owner of the house was on his way out to prey on less fortunate beings. He needed to move fast. Brian entered the home. The door was unlocked as he knew it would be. He had removed his tie and let it dangle from his hand. The occupant of the home had heard him come in and called out. "Is that you, Vicki?" Brian waited in the corner of the kitchen at the foot of the stairs until the man came down. He grabbed his shoulders and pulled him into the kitchen.

"You!" The man yelled as Brian looped the tie around his neck and pulled it tighter and tighter until the victim's eyes enlarged. The veins in his neck swelled. The older man tried to reach the knife block on the counter but was pulled to the floor. His face turned blue. He struck Brian's face, but it was a weak blow from someone whose life was being wrung out of him, second by slow second. The tension on the tie was maintained until the struggling stopped. Blood-shot eyeballs stared back at him in disbelief, dismay and shock. His gnarled fingers still gripped Brian's shirt.

The bile rose in his gullet. He rushed to the washroom and retched into the toilet bowl, flushed, washed his face in the sink and returned to the kitchen. The crumpled heap on the floor was well-known. Recently, the television stations had shown the grieving man who had lost his wife the previous week when a home burglary had apparently led to murder. The husband's tearful pleadings for information leading to the killer elicited enough support in the city. Brian wanted to vomit again but controlled himself. *How could this have happened? How could he possibly have done something like this?* But, it was strange. He felt no regret. Rather he felt at peace. It was odd. A relief. He exhaled slowly. *How could he feel this way after what he had done?* He was not a violent man. On the contrary this was totally out of character for him. His mother would have been shocked by his actions. They had cared so much for each other. He wished he had never left home but then, after graduation, he had to. It was in his teenage years when the troubles had begun.

The phone was on the kitchen counter. It was time to make the call. He hoped he would feel better when they came. "There's been a... an... accident." Brian heard himself say. He gave the address. Shortly thereafter an ambulance and a squad car arrived at the home. The door was opened. Two officers entered. After they saw the corpse on the kitchen floor, the officers gestured for him to move away from the body. A forensic team arrived after one of the officers phoned. Crime scene tape was placed around the home. Curious neighbours had already gathered on the other side of the street after having heard the police sirens and seen the flashing lights. They were already talking to reporters who had also shown up as they often do in situations like this. Brian was driven to the police station after he told the officers what had happened.

A man in a grey suit led him to a small room and beckoned him to sit at one of the two metal chairs around a rectangular table which held two plastic bottles of water. The concrete walls were painted white. A bright overhead light hung over the table. At the top of one of the corners of the room was a video camera. A red light was blinking on the camera.

"You are shivering. Do you need a blanket?" Brian shook his head. "Are you sure you don't want to call your lawyer?" He sat at one corner of the desk, close to Brian. He pointed to the camera in the corner to indicate that their conversation was being recorded.

"No. I don't need one. I did what needed to be done."

"That sounds like a confession to me. Brian, are you sure you don't need to call your lawyer? This is a very serious matter. You don't appear to be drunk or on drugs. You have no previous record. But if that's what you want, let's talk about what happened in a little bit more detail."

Talk? Of course, he would talk. He would tell him everything. The phone calls late at night. The sound of women crying on the other end of the line. The shouts. The arguments and the berating. The sleepless nights. But he would relate, in detail, his nightmare of a woman whom he had loved who had been strangled in her own bed. He could hear the shouting and sometimes the sound of thumping on the other side of his bedroom wall. A woman weeping, crying, begging for mercy. Perhaps it was a nightmare from his youth. He wasn't sure. But his head pounded. He wanted to do something but he couldn't. The door to his bedroom was locked from the outside. He was trapped!

"Brian, Brian. Are you with me? Do you need some more time? Do you know what you have done?"

"Yes, I do. My father had it coming. He killed my mother last week. I'm dead certain."

Three Kings and a Joker

"You idiot! I don't want to deal with you anymore! I am no longer your agent!" He slammed the phone down and sprang from his desk. Enough was enough! He needed a change. A big change. There was something missing in his life. He had to find it. There was only one way.

Helmet clipped to his stout chin, his Harley roared to life. An unseen force pulled the bike south, along the grey asphalt streak through the foothills. The streak took his mind back to the days he had streaked at Wimbledon. Thereafter, his friends called him 'Mr. Bojangles'.

His travelling companion, Rob, who was also seeking a change, hung back at a safe distance. He knew our hero would lead the way. Maybe not to Salvation, but at least to some good drinking establishments...

Up ahead our protagonist could see a shape in the middle of the lane. It was a grizzly! Fortunately, Lady Luck had placed a bump in the road which allowed our man to fly over the head of the voracious carnivore. The grizzly looked up, confused. It loved Meals on Wheels and this was an opportunity missed. Our hero shook his head in disbelief. *Someone up there must be looking after me...*

He was sure now that he was on the right track to self realization as he powered down the highway. Rob stayed at an even safer distance, after having missed the grizzly, barely. The wind was at our protagonist's back. Eating beans for breakfast gave his bike that extra oomph. Rob stayed at an even safer distance behind. Ahead he could see a sign. It was not the sign he was looking for, but it was close enough: *Eureka, the friendliest town, on the loneliest road in America.*

Our man was lonely and needed a friend. His focused mind had removed the presence of Rob who was still a safe distance behind. His sharp mind flashed back to his childhood:

"Why am I here?" he remembered asking when he was a small child...At that time the answer was "because you live here..." His father had a great sense of humour.

Back to the present. And his mission. The Omen was there. A town called Eureka would be the first stop on the road to self realization. After he parked his bike, he looked around, but there was no apple tree, and no apple about to fall on his head. A grave situation, but not totally devoid of gravity. Newton would have been disappointed, but not our hero...

His hot Harley was cooling in the shade of the only tree in Eureka. His keen eyes noticed a shady figure seated on a porch outside a red saloon. Soundlessly our man edged closer to the swinging half-doors near where the cowboy seemingly dozed on a bench. Looking out of the corner of his eagle eye he was expecting to be challenged. His large frame was wound up like a clock-spring. The figure on the bench didn't move.

Mannequins are like that...

Our hero's broad shoulders nudged the door open. "Can someone get a drink in here?" He asked.

"Someone can, but not you," a female voice answered. He looked to his left. There she was. A Dolly Parton look-alike. A low-cut crimson blouse framing her essentials. Both of them. Being more of a good writer than a voyeur, his mind immediately flashed back to Hemingway's novel: *For Whom the Balls Toil.* Was that the title? Never mind...

"What brings you here, you devilish man?" She sidled up to our man, stroking his helmet, which was now protecting his crotch. He didn't trust women making the first move. In fact, he recalled his last move. It was from England to Canada...

Here he was in the United States of America. Is this where he belonged? "I'm no devil. I'm just Canadian," he responded, dryly.

"Canada Dry, no doubt?"

"I can use one." Our hero was thirsty indeed.

"Do you want a shot of something in that?" Dolly look-a-like asked.

"What's your name?" He figured being friendly wouldn't hurt. No point picking a fight so early in his self realization trip.

Especially a fight with someone who was so up front, if you know what I mean? He thought cleverly.

"I have to spend some time in the desert. I have to be alone." His hypnotic stare fixed on the ice cube in his glass, rather than on a more interesting place, like the Valley of the Dolly.

"Did you know there was someone following you?"

Our hero spun around. "Rob! How nice to see you!"

"We were in this together buddy..."

"Oh, I had forgotten. You didn't mind my dust, did you?"

"The dust was the least of my problems. Somethin' was stinkin' in them thar hills," responded Rob, cowboying up.

They sat down to look at the menu which Dolly gave them. Rob grimaced at the menu:

Beans and Brocolli: $4.99

Beans and Cabbage: $4.99

Beans and Sprouts: $4.99

Beans: 50 cents

"Huh, why is that?"

"Because we have a large Beanstalk in the back."

"I hope you got Jack off," Rob laughed.

"Please, no trash talk. I'm a born-again Christmastime." Dolly said coldly.

"You mean 'Christian'," corrected Rob.

"I meant want I said, and I have the baubles to prove it," Dolly answered, pointedly.

Our hero shook his head. He hurriedly ate his plate of beans. Now that he was gassed up he knew he had important things to do. Like his date with Destiny. No, not Beyonce of Destiny's Child, but his destiny. Beyonce would have to wait her turn...it was time to move on. But our champion wanted to be alone for the remainder of his trip. Rob didn't mind staying behind with Dolly. Her real name was Dolly La Valley. He was taken by her posture. But then, so was our hero.

His Harley bellowed to life. A cloud of desert dust was all that Rob and Dolly could see as he disappeared over the horizon, while Rob rested his head on Dolly's breast. Quite the Rest Stop....

The sun was slowly setting behind the Sierra Nevada Mountains. A golden glow suffused the valley. The stars began peeking from the sky as the warm desert wind subsided. Our man peered closely since the road was getting more difficult to navigate in the near darkness. He could hear predators howling on the other side of the rise in the road.

Suddenly a comet blazed across the heavens, making him slow down to watch in awe and expectation. A bright star danced on the horizon and seemed to be coming nearer to him. Closer and closer. He could no longer hear the roar of his Harley and could not feel its pulsating engine. The bike was floating above the desert floor. Unexpectedly he was at the top of a mountain. An unseen hand seemed to have lifted him to the mountain top.

Must have been the beans our hero thought. But it wasn't. Ahead in the gloom he could see shadows moving towards him. Closer they came. Icicles ran up and down his shivering spine. The desert air began to warm around him and suddenly he was bathed in a shaft of intense light from above. The star was directly above him!

"Hello, Michael."

"Hi, Mike."

"Hey-O, Mikey."

Into the shaft of light walked three large figures clothed in black leather chaps with chrome studs. Hairy, tattooed arms burst from their tank tops.

"Who are you?" He asked with trepidation. He didn't like trepidation. He preferred consternation, since he was a writer of some repute.

The large men looked at him.

"You must know us," one said.

"I'm sorry. We have not been introduced." His keen sense of etiquette, developed from many years in fine schools, had taught him that introductions were essential prior to conversation.

"We are the three Kings."

"Kings?!"

"Yes. We are Cole, Frankinstead and Muir."

Mike looked closely at the apparition in the middle. It did look a bit like Frankenstein. There was definitely a bolt through his head. A dead bolt.

"We are the Kings Crew. We have advice for you," Cole said.

"Sometink you will like, Master..." said Frankinstead.

"Wot you've always wanted, but more of the same..." volunteered Muir.

Mike pinched himself. This could not be happening to him. Three Kings, in the desert, in a shaft of light from above...

"I don't believe..." he started to say.

"But you must believe," Cole stated.

"Yes, you must, to enter..." said Frankinstead.

"The Kingdom," Muir advised.

Mike dismounted his bike, anxiety tearing his heart out of his chest.

"Am I dead?"

"You are very much alive." Cole confirmed.

"Full of Life," Frankinstead added.

"Never looked better," Muir whispered.

"So what Kingdom am I about to enter?" Our puzzled hero asked. This time without trepidation. By the way, he did miss his *Intrepid*, the only car he had ever owned.

"The Kingdom of Wisdom," the Three Kings chorused.

"Does that mean I must leave this earth?"

"Oh no. Not just yet," said King Cole. Nattily. His velvet voice reminded Mike of someone else...

Frankinstead pushed the bolt out the other side of his head. "You will remain on earth, Master."

Muir nodded his head. "Down to earth. On Earth."

Nervousness overcame Mike and his knees started to knock. He reached for the smokes in his vest pocket. A very special type of cigarette. He offered these to the three kings.

They shook their heads. "Weed rather not."

Rings of smoke swirled around Mike.

"Tell me more..." he asked calmly. *Amazing what that tobacco can do for your nerves.*

"You must go back," said Cole.

"To where you came from, Master," added Frankinstead.

"To whom you belong to," Muir advised.

"Where to, and who to?"

"Eureka. To her," they chorused.

"What?"

"Not 'what'," Cole said, emphatically.

"But you know who, Master."

Muir broke into song. "Lavender Blue, Dolly Dolly, Lavender Blue."

"You mean Lavender Blue, Dilly Dilly," corrected Mike, always the perfect lyricist.

"That's up to you, what you do with your Dilly. But you need Dolly for that."

The three Kings nodded wisely.

"But why?" Mike asked. This time with apprehension.

"Dolly is your Present," said Cole, with intensity.

"And your Future, Master," said Frankinstead, with finality.

"She makes your Future Perfect," said Muir. (He liked to be grammatically correct).

The figures immediately dissolved into smoke before his eyes. The shaft of light disappeared as quickly as it had come.

Darkness enveloped our champion. The bike was back on the desert floor. Engine warm, but soundless. The scent of lavender encircled him. They were gone, as suddenly as they had come. Mike turned his bike around and sped back down the road. To Eureka. Three Kings could not be wrong. He sang Lavender Blue Dilly Dilly as he felt a surge of youth transform his body.

Well, not all of it, but at least one of the body parts, where life was beginning to take form...

A Brief History of Mine

A few years ago, I read Stephen Hawking's book *A Brief History of Time*. I understood very little of it. To fill my immense knowledge gap of mathematics and numbers, I did intensive research at the Okotoks Library where the books on Science filled exactly one-eighth of one bookshelf. But the book I found was astounding.

My study of numbers and the great mathematicians and scientists took me back to BC. Not British Columbia (those scumbags who don't want our pipelines) but Before Christmas. Not the last one, but the first one. And it was in this massive one-inch tome that I found that the study of math may have begun in early India (well before BBC: Before Brits Came, or, Before Bastards Came, as was said in more acrimonious states, where residents hated acronyms and the Brits).

On page 23 of this valuable contribution to history, entitled *The History of Everything and Then Some* by Frederick the Fake, was a story of a Hindu mystic.

One day, the mystic was chilling out on the banks of the Ganges smoking something powerful, as all mystic do. In his highly altered state, he observed that all around him were flowers of many types. He deeply inhaled more magic mushroom smoke, and discovered that the flowers had one, three, five, eight or thirteen petals. Nature could be explained with numbers with a certain sequence. The third number was the sum of the previous two and this continued in a somewhat natural sequence. One, Three, Five, Eight, Thirteen. That was an astounding discovery. Even for a mystic. Let's call him Misty for simplicity.

Misty butted out and ran to his wife, yelling. (By the way, the wife of a mystic is called a Mistake). But since they were politically correct even in those days, he would call her 'Ms.' She found that hard to take, but tolerated the old goat anyway.

"One, three, five, eight? So what?" She yelled. "Why don't you do something useful, like feeding the chickens?" He told her patiently that he had just done the grass. He strolled away, half clothed, as they always were in those days. Because at that time they had 'fifty-percent-off' sales which everyone took advantage of, even the mystics.

Misty decided to record his findings on a large plantain leaf which he then floated down the Ganges. It was a sacred river and would take his discovery to someone who would recognize its significance. He went back to his business of doing the usual. You know: meditating, stretching and gazing into space. This type of activity was also ground-breaking. In the future, business opportunities would abound for thousands of fake yogis in North America, who would actually charge good money for stretching and posing in the most ridiculous ways, in poses called 'Downward Dog' and 'Up Yours'.

The plantain leaf's journey on the Ganges took it to the Indian Ocean. The currents carried it to the coast of Italy where it was buried in the sand for centuries.

A young man by the name of Fibonacci, who lived in Naples and worked in a flower shop, loved to walk along the beach, smoking the same magic mushrooms Misty smoked more than a thousand years before. His sandals got caught on something in the sand. (Sandals often get caught in the sand, which is there). Then he noticed this plantain leaf with the strange inscriptions. Fibonacci was very well-read. (They had a library in Naples similar to the one in the future progressive town of Okotoks). He was able to understand the scrawls of numbers and something struck him. It wasn't a coconut. In case you didn't know, they didn't have any coconut trees in Naples. Despite future flavours of ice cream and candy being called Neapolitan Coconut. Naples was never called Neaples.

Fibonacci had often wondered why, when his mother sliced pizza, she would only cut it into two, four or eight pieces. Now he fully understood this message from the past. With plantain leaf in hand he picked up some flowers from the flower shop and ran home to mama.

"Mama, mama," he shouted excitedly. Even in year 1400 the Italians shouted instead of talking quietly, like the Dapper Duke of Dunsmuir.

"Watta you gone and done? Did you leave-a the flower shop without closing up again? You stoopid boy! You know dat Romeo will come and take alla da flowers for dat stoopid Julietta again. Go back to the flower shop otherwise I won't washa your clothes anymore. And when they invent the Iron I won't iron them eedda." She was a very forward-thinking person. Definitely ahead of her time. Like her son.

Fibonacci tried to explain to his mama that all the flowers had either one, three, five, eight or thirteen petals. He showed her the ancient plantain leaf inscriptions written by

Misty. She hit him on the side of his head and sent him back to the flower shop. His mother took the plantain leaf and dumped spaghetti and meatballs on it. She served it to Professor Ladeeze Zumano who was visiting her. Her husband, Cornuto, was away doing research in the City of Lights. Red Lights. The professor ate his meal in silence because his mind was only on one thing, like most mathematicians: the numbers 38-22-36. After the meal and a lengthy discourse, followed by a short intercourse (very short), he turned to leave but then noticed the plantain leaf. He asked his hostess if he could take it home as a souvenir of the fulfilling visit. Instead of taking it home however, he placed it on the wall of his office at the University of Firenze. He coated it with a clear paste to preserve the important sequence of numbers which he grudgingly named the Fibonnaci sequence. He was, after all, the little idiot's father.

Its secret may have been there for centuries had it not been for Professor Figginbotham from Friggintown University. The professor, while having a cup of tea (which he had introduced to the Italian after the recent plundering of China by his countrymen), asked if he could make a drawing of that artwork on the wall of Professor Ladeeze Zumano. He carefully drew this sequence of numbers and took the drawing back to his university. He placed it on the desk of his secretary, who he was having an affair with, and forgot all about it. She kept the drawing as a memento. After all, she had lost count after the first eight times of illicit love-making. Was it eight, thirteen or twenty-one times? It didn't matter. It was consensual and sequential.

Alas, she later gave birth to a young boy. Out of wedlock. In remembrance of Professor Figginbotham, whom she often called Figg, she named the boy Figg-Newton and gave him the drawing the professor had made.

When the boy grew up he ran away from home, because he could not stand being called a figging bastard by his farm friends. He dropped the name Figg when he entered the prestigious University of Cambridge, well known for its fruitless research. Newton was not a social person and couldn't give a fig for any friendships. He often sat under the apple tree lost in thought. He would sometimes fall asleep but one day was awoken by a thump on his head. He awoke to see who had struck him, but no one was around. He was about to doze off when another thump woke him up. Then he noticed that an apple had fallen on his head. This was an omen from above, that his life would not be fruitless.

"This is a very grave situation," he said to himself. "Very grave. Grave, grave, grave. Hey, I get it now! Grave, grave. Gravity!" He rushed back to his office, pulled out the Fibonacci series of numbers from his desk and wrote down an additional mathematical law. The Law of Gravity. 'Earth sucks'. There's no escape. This was a ground-breaking finding. But he dared not break any more ground because gravity would thereby increase. Gravity sucks, remember?

For the next few centuries some accomplishments took place in Europe but then the Germans coaxed some citizens to move on. Europe was no longer a place for peaceful co-existence and all that shit. One of the emigres, who was born on March 14, 1879, left for the shores of America in the 1930's.

He began his work immersed in numbers, the Fibonacci Series, gravity and the mathematical term, Pi. He was not interested in the unresolved question of how many digits there were in Pi, since it was too long-drawn-out answer. One day, while Einstein was eating the American version of Pie, he looked up and said: "Oh heavens, what have we up there?"

It was like a light bulb that went off in his head. His hair pointed in all directions, (which it did for the rest of his life), and he quickly wrote down the formula '$E=mc^2$'. Wow! He was on to something but nobody knew what it was, not even his wife, who was in the dark about all his affairs anyway. But he surmised that gravity affected time and space. The farther you travelled from earth's gravity the slower you would age. But then he couldn't escape earth's gravity and died peacefully in Princeton, New Jersey.

And to think all these profound discoveries started with a Hindu mystic smoking weed...

The light story may be a good way to illustrate the value of science and mathematics to some people. I hope that in the future, scientists and mathematicians will enjoy the same social status as some of today's 'celebrities'.

Not the Final Frontier

Most of us here today are nomads. We have always been nomads. But we need to prepare for a journey that is truly out of this world. When food and water is scarce we move on to find another oasis. Another place to stay, albeit temporarily, until the well runs dry. No water. No life. Then we move again, in search of the next oasis. This cycle has been repeated for many centuries but now the land and its gifts are not enough to sustain our population of seven billion people. Is our number up?

Mankind has experienced drought, plague, famine, volcanic eruptions, fires, floods and storms. In the past we have risen from these events and thrived. But as the population grows, so do conflicts. The potential for an accidental or intentional nuclear war has grown. With our vast number of weapons, mechanical, biological and chemical, there is little chance that these will not be used in the near future on much larger scales that we have seen before. Is our number up?

Population growth has been the result of the great advances we have made in sciences. These great advances include agriculture and medicine. Fewer people die of hunger or illness today than in previous centuries. Our little planet may have a lot of land but it is being exploited today, not only for intensive farming, but also for those valuable minerals such as coal, oil, metals and, of course, gold.

For a few pounds of gold for rings, necklaces and bracelets, many tons of earth are excavated. Tons of fresh water is used to purify this metal. For those cellphones, the same is true. There are rare earth minerals that are required to make these. Consequently, many more tons of earth get excavated and the water gets contaminated. We call it progress. But we live in a fishbowl which is getting murkier and murkier. The nomads always found pure water and breathed clean air. But that is not in our future. Instead, it is in our past. Is our number up?

Nowadays, the water we drink and the air we breathe has more contaminants in it than in previous times. The Mariana trench, the deepest ocean trench, was thought to be free of contamination. Unfortunately, polychlorinated biphenyls (PCBs) have been found there, as they have been found in the fat of our majestic whales and polar bears. Most of the drinking water in our cities, the stuff of life, is a cocktail including micro-plastics, estrogens, spent antibiotics and other chemicals which pose significant health risks to current and future populations of people, plants and animals. These cannot be removed by water treatment plants. Our population has exploded to over seven billion people and we are now living longer that our parents or grandparents. We have to find more living space. We are running out. Is our number up?

There are swaths of land that are no longer habitable due to nuclear testing, wars and accidents that have occurred in Russia, the US and Japan. A huge lake in Russia was contaminated due to nuclear testing. If anyone entered that lake they would be dead within ten minutes. Clear, pristine looking water, ready to claim the next victim.

The earth has been hit by large meteorites before, and is still in a cosmic shooting gallery. The result will be that our earth will survive, as it has for millennia, but we, as a species will not. It is time to move on. To the heavens. Yes, our number is up.

Once again, our knowledge of the sciences will hopefully rescue us. But not in the way that it has before. The science of numbers and mathematics as we know it, was born in India approximately thirteen hundred years ago and has provided us the foundation to plan our next move. Great thinkers at that time developed a system of numbers which was part of the ancient Hindu religion.

This system of numbers was called Hindu/Arabic. If you think Math is horrid, remember that it could have been the Roman numeral system that Europe adopted.

Fibonacci was one of the mathematicians who made the Hindu/Arabic numeral system popular. The sequence of numbers that bear his name is the Fibonacci series. In this series, every third number is the sum of the two previous numbers. For example, zero plus one is one. One plus two is three and three plus two is five. So, the sequence is: one, three, five, eight, thirteen and so on. This parallels nature, and is perhaps what had been noted by a Hindu mystic in ancient India. Flowers have one, three, five or eight petals. Exactly per the mathematical series. The number of seeds in sunflowers and pinecones add up to a number in the Fibonacci series.

When you work from a seed in the centre of a sunflower and follow a clockwise- spiral outwards, you will end up with a Fibonacci number. The same number if you follow the spiral counter-clockwise. These spirals can be observed if you slice a cabbage in half, of if you look at certain sea-shells.

Mathematics and numbers led to the exploration of the heavens. Galileo looked through a telescope and found that the earth was not the centre of the universe. He was imprisoned for this heresy and served the rest of his life within the walls of his own home. Galileo died on January 8, 1642. Three hundred years later, also on January 8, Stephen Hawking was born, in 1942. Coincidentally Hawking died on March 14, 2018 and March 14 was the date that Albert Einstein was born.

Are these dates and numbers coincidental? Or is it destined that great minds share the same dates? Is there a connection to the universe with these numbers? There is symmetry of numbers in sunflowers, pinecones, trees, animals and humans. This has prompted a scientist to write a book *Is God a Mathematician?* Do numbers neatly describe everything in our universe?

Galileo, Newton, Einstein and Hawking were all trying to explain the mystery of the Universe to us based on mathematics and numbers. Stephen Hawking developed several hard-to-understand mathematical formulae that point to the existence of black holes in our, and other, galaxies. Hawking was working on one formula to explain the universe but has now left it to others to determine what that formula is. But all of them, looked to the heavens. They all likely knew that one day we will have to move on like the nomads. And perhaps heaven can help us. Because our number is up.

The launch of *Sputnik* in 1957 was a first step. Subsequently we developed the Apollo spacecraft and visited the moon. Then we built a space station the size of a football field which weighs a million tons and spins around the earth at more than seventeen-thousand miles per hour.

Several missions have been flown to the International Space Station and hundreds of astronauts have been our guinea pigs to test the adaptability of the human body to weightlessness, being bombarded by cosmic radiation and living in close quarters with other crew members without conflict. These brave souls have shown that the absence of gravity leads to rapid loss of bone density, vision, balance and DNA changes.

But, without this knowledge and experience, we cannot venture out farther into space. During these first steps many animals and humans have died, but the exploration must continue if we are to survive as a race. Or else the only record of our existence will be on a CD with two hundred hours of recordings of videos and pictures of living things on our planet. Our music and many languages are also on this CD. *Voyager 1*, which carries this CD, was launched in 1977. It left our solar system in 2015. It is now 13 billion miles away from Earth. At this distance, light and radio signals take nineteen hours to be received.

The Hubble space telescope that was launched in 1990 has looked deep into space and has confirmed that our tiny solar system is really a speck of dust in the universe. There are millions of other galaxies and thousands of planets similar to earth that we can live on. We need to move on.

Stephen Hawking, the big man in the wheelchair, fought a brave fight with Lou Gehrig's disease for more than fifty years. He is one of the many scientists who agree that we need to have a Plan B. Another place to live, since our planet will not be hospitable for humans.

On a moonless night look up at the black sky. Thousands of points of light can be seen with the naked eye. With the Hubble telescope we have seen trillions of celestial bodies. Some twinkling and others constant. In that vast, seemingly endless place, where will we find a home? It is up there. In the future, like in our past, we will become nomads again.

There is not doubt that our number is up.

Stones with Stories

Stones tell stories. Many stories. Some are joyous and filled with laughter. Others tinged with hate and evil. I was at a place today with many rocks. They were gray, white, or black. And some green, but these were not jade.

Rocks are living things. They are cold and still. They are old. Very, very old. Despite their age they can still speak. Each had a tale to tell. And I was keen to listen.

I was in an old city. Built on rocks. A city somewhat less in age than the rocks, but an age of at least several centuries. These stones have had the ice of winter scar their smooth faces. The winds of spring, laden with sand, have honed their rough edges. The warmth of the summer sun is stored in the stones. The heat is given to other living things.

Plants root in the earth by the rocks. They bloom and blossom. Mosses flourish on their kind faces. The palette of green, red and gold begins to brown. Another sleep through winter is nigh. Before the next renewal. The birth and then the death.

There was in deep silence where I now stood. Then the blackbirds, robins and starlings broke this stillness with their melodious calls. It was a place of peace. And meditation. And memories of long ago that have not been forgotten.

I paused at a white rock. The carving said 'Angels never die'. I asked 'Why is that?' My gaze moved down to a small green bottle among the stones. *Jagermeister*. The birds stopped singing. I felt cold. Angry. Fearful. In my mind, I started to scream. And then to cry. Then I was angry again. No. Furious. I was in a bad place. I retreated quickly.

I left the rock which had unlocked its terrifying past. I moved to another. A black one. The birdsong resumed. I heard children laughing. And then shrieking. Some moments of silence. And then again laughter. Lots of laughter. A chorus of giggles and chuckles. And then the sound of a child snoring. On my shoulder. I could not help but cry.

It had been so long ago when I had been a young father. The rock seemed to smile as well. It seemed to crackle like a slow burning log in a fireplace radiating warmth, comfort and love. I looked at the engraving on the rock. There were two names: Jakob and Wilhelm. They must have been brothers. I smiled. I knew them. Well. Very well. Like so many of us. I bowed and said my thanks to them. Their rocks had told me so many stories.

Now I must leave this refuge. The area around was once a mountain of rubble. Caused by the black birds that had fallen from the sky. The earth had trembled. Magnificent edifices of this great city were shattered as were so many lives. But then, when the sound of thunder had dissipated and the dust had settled, the city was reborn.

The children are laughing again. But in the quiet place in the city, many are beneath the rocks. In their final resting place, below the stooping branches of trees filled with cherries and apples, and the full-throated warbles of jays, finches and robins.

J.G. Barrie

The cemetery in Berlin was consecrated in 1856. It is called Alter St. Matthus Kirchof (Old St. Matthews Churchyard).

The first gravestone I visited was very recent. It was placed there in 2015. It is the gravestone of a very prominent Hells Angel. The second grave, circa 1860, belonged to The Brothers Grimm.

Dark and Light share the same plot of land.

It's Spring Again

Hey, its me again. Al. I guess you want to know what I've been doin' all winter. Well, it was shovel, shovel, shovel. You know how it is, eh? Snows all night, and there's me, the last one on the block wakin' up to shovel all that shit... jeez.

Why do we need to shovel, eh? Let Ol' Mother Nature do it for us, is my suggestion. So what if yer basement or garage gets flooded? It's only water, eh? Besides, why have so much stuff in the garage or basement in the first place, eh? All I got is a few cases of beer, well, maybe more that a few, but anyways that's all I got in my garage. And of course, used oil from the times I've changed my oil. A few gallon drums, eh. One of these days I'll take it to the dump.

Oh yeah, of course all those empties are also in my garage. Like pop bottles. Minnie loves diet Coke and I love my beer, eh. Between us there's lotsa containers, eh? But what the hell, gotta enjoy life eh? What's wrong with a few drinks now and then, especially when I'm watchin' hockey while Minnie does errands for Bert. Poor Bert. Not the same after that accident, eh.

Where wuz I? Oh, yeah. Winter and shovelling. Thank God its over, eh? Now we got Spring again. You know the first sign of spring that I notice? Them house flies. Lots of them in my kitchen. All of a sudden they're buzzin around like cats out of Hell, eh? Don't know where they hibernate, maybe under the kitchen sink. But that's strange since I take out the garbage regular like, eh. Once a month is plenty, eh? Anyhow, maybe flies don't hibernate. Maybe they lay eggs. I dunno. Too scientific for me. Gotta ask Bert about it one of these days...

Where wuz I? Oh yeah, shovelling, eh? Had to do it yesterday cos my truck got stuck on ice. Lotsa ice. Betcha it was about six inches under the truck. Can't understand how so much collects there, eh? Maybe that's why my neighbours shovel often. Wish I had thought of that earlier.

Anyways, so my truck wheels were spinnin' away after I tried to move, eh? An' I said to myself. Now what can I do bout this? So, I had this great idea. I jacked up the truck, eh. Put some old oil pans under the rear wheels (my truck is one of them rear-wheel- drive types for you that don't know mechanical stuff like I do...). Anyways, so I lowered the jack, real slow, eh. Can never be too careful eh? Especially when the engines a'runnin. I did have it in neutral, eh. Cos I'm a mechanical type guy as you know...

Anyways so I remove the jacks, eh, and the wheels sit down real pretty on them waste oil pans. They were kinda clean eh. So I get into the truck and put it into reverse. Holy cow, did I get a shock! Them oil pans came aflyin' out from the bottom and smashed into my basement winder glass. I turned the engine off reel quick, eh, to survey the damage. Fortunately, I found some cardboard in the garage and closed off the winder so it wouldn't get too cold, eh. Figured I'd just go and get me some more beer and hot dogs and stuff and come back reel quick to fix the winder better.

But when I put the truck in reverse again, a whole bunch of oil came a spinnin' out since the tires had picked up some from the oil pan. The truck tires flung the oil against my cardboard winder protection and now it was adrippin' onto the driveway somethin' bad, eh.

Truck wouldn't go nowhere, eh, so I put it in neutral and pushed it onto the road. Wish I had thought of that before. Or maybe the oil and ice made it easier to push. So I get into the truck, start her up and I'm off. Then I came to the Stop Sign. And it wouldn't stop! There was still oil on them tires. So I slide through the Stop Sign, eh, and next thing I know the front end of my truck breaks through the neighbour's garage and smashes into his brand new Dodge Ram! Ah shit! I thought, what will I do now?

So I get out and knock on his door. Nobody home, eh. So I thought it would be nice to leave him a note, eh. I didn't have a pen or paper in my truck so I figured there may be some paper and a pen in his house. So I open the door, eh? All of us leave our doors open, eh? This is Canada, eh?

Across the livin' room I see a pad of paper in his kitchen, by his phone. So I call out, just to be sure he ain't home. He wasn't. I walk over and write the note: 'Please call. Sorry about your truck. I will fix it in the shop.' I wrote down Bert's phone number since I don't have a phone.

When I turned around I noticed that oil from my boots was all over his white rug. Think it was Persian or something from outside Alberta. *Darn!* I said. *I'd better fix this too.* So I went back to the kitchen and wrote. Sorry about the rug, I will fix that too. And then I walked out. But before I left, I noticed that I had put a second set of oily prints on his rug. Aww shucks, gimme a break, eh.

Now I'm outside. I put my truck in reverse. And you know what? It's the same guy, returnin' with his brand-new

Tesla. And, once again, I couldn't stop. Well, the guy was fit to be hog-tied. He screamed at me reel bad and I couldn't get a word in lengthwise, or is it 'edge-wise'? Anyways, you know what I mean...

When I was driving away, he opened his door, saw his rug and started hollerin' again. I honked and waved back to him. Hey, I don't wanna be hard on my neighbours, eh? Especially when spring has sprung.

The Children of Conflict

The Leader he stood
In the far distant wood
He called for the soldiers so brave
To fight to the death
Till their last gasp of breath
With guns so cold in the grave

The children at play
Not far from the bay
Heard drums and bagpipes a-sounding
They looked up and saw
With fear, shivers and awe
As black birds from above came a-bounding

The homes and the houses
Of children and spouses
Of men-folk at work in the field
Exploded with force
That cut off discourse
As blood in their throats was congealed

The hands and the feet
Of the children so sweet
Flew up in the air with the gust
And mothers cried
As infants had died
While soldiers did what they must

J.G. Barrie

And the Leader was praised
As the village was razed
To the ground midst the gathering gloom
But the cheers were loud
For the leader so proud
And the man who was Master of Doom

It's children like these
Who are brought to their knees
By leaders so vile and so greedy
Who give not a damn
And live in a sham
As the children who die are the Needy

And the cycle goes on
Hither and yon
In the hills and the valleys and stubble
As men lust for power
And toddlers cower
In their homes that are now only rubble

Through forests they weave
Once full of blossom and leave
Now craters and smoke and ember
But the borders were closed
Which they never supposed
For death awaits in December

The guard at the gate
Laughs along with his mate
As they survey the bony and ashen
And their children throw stones
And the multitude moans
For mercy and food and compassion

And the Leader so bold
With his heart oh so cold
Demands that the soldiers do take
The boys and the girls
Still in their curls
As servants and slaves he will make

And the Children of War
Year after year suffer more
As Leaders with anger preach hate
Young lives torn asunder
The children they wonder
Is Death and Destruction their fate?

The Last Battle

It was time. My wife puckered up for that farewell kiss and waved from the doorway as I pulled away. I wish she could have been with me. But I was going to a place where you wouldn't want to take your loved one. "I'll be back soon, honey."

You can call me a veteran. I deserve that honour. But once again, I was being drawn into battle. Would I survive this one, like I had so many others? This was the fight that hopefully would not be my last. I recall that the training had been intense when I was younger. We would all be awoken at five o'clock in the morning and would begin gruelling marches of two miles, carrying backpacks that seemed to weigh as much as each of us did. Then there were obstacle courses to be covered in a limited time, river crossings when the river was in full flow, rope ladders to be climbed and the repetitive drag and lift of what seemed like hundreds of sandbags. Our day would end an hour before midnight. But that was when I was much younger...

The battle which was to begin would be far more dangerous. Hence, we had hired a former sergeant to whip our company into shape. We called him Sergeant Croc and he relished that nickname. But he was truly a man of steel and Kevlar. He had survived three vicious battles a year for the last seven years. The scars could be seen on his arms, his legs and his leathery face. A piece of his ear was missing, some teeth lost. When he grinned, which was seldom, he bared two large incisors that could likely match those of a cobra. But he was not a Charmer. Rather, a snake. Sleek, speedy and stealthy. All the attributes of a victor.

The day dawned on a very pleasant November morning. But was this a good day to die? I put on my boots, my padded vest, hat and fatigues. Others in my company did the same. We walked grim-faced into the battleground knowing that the enemy was not them, but us. Yes, at a time like this, feelings of remorse and fear sometimes come to the fore. But we had planned well ahead for this battle. We had gathered the intelligence from others who had been in that place and we knew, very well, how the land lay. Certainly not the hallowed ground of yesteryear. But a place for battle no doubt. We had talked to veterans of previous conflicts and had gleaned from them nuggets of information that we would certainly use. What to watch for. The importance of cunning, agility and keeping the senses on high alert. Not to depend on the tools that we had been provided, but instead to use our senses. See like an eagle, smell like a beagle and listen like a lynx. And of course, to depend on that 'gut feeling': intuition.

The clock was running down. We were ready to charge. And charge we did. The enemy vastly outnumbered us. But we pushed forward. We had to gain the vantage point before they took it. They would not stop us. We had courage, resolve and most of all, conviction. There was a rumble. Shouts. Screams. In anger and agony. Fists flailed and curses were hurled. Bloodied faces smiled with satisfaction or cowed in shame. The horde advanced but we held our ground. Suddenly my knees buckled. I was losing it. After all that training I had become the prey! I had lost. Where there was light was now blackness. Memories ebbed and flowed. Voices loud, but then soft.

I woke up in a hospital. My wife was there, shaking her head. "You are too old for this. It's time you stopped attending Black Friday Sales, Marius."

A Good Man

Sailing ships, buffeted by the Trade Winds, visited Pondicherry. It became the headquarters of the French East India Company in the seventeenth century. Baroque buildings and dwellings dotted the coastal areas of this quaint city. The French influence also permeated our family tree. Perhaps a soldier or a trader, by the name of Barré, mingled with a brown-skinned native beauty on the beach by the Bay of Bengal one romantic summer evening. My father was born in Hubli, on the western coast of India, but his ancestors likely came from Pondicherry. He was one of five children. His mother died during childbirth. His father later married his sister-in-law whom the children referred to as 'Non'.

I never had lengthy discussions with my father. In two decades he said little about his childhood. Perhaps he didn't want to discuss his humble beginnings. Frugality was a necessity in his youthful years. There also had to be a reason for his generosity and selflessness. Growing up with siblings who were malnourished had likely created a lasting influence on my father. He chastised us if we wasted food and often said 'Waste Not. Want Not'. He told us that, when he was young, his family was so hungry that his brothers and sisters would eat grass. Perhaps that is why I was so profoundly affected by a scene in the movie *Gone with the Wind* when Scarlett Ohara pulled a radish out of the soil and chomped on it like a famished rabbit. She swore *'As God is my witness, I will never be hungry again.'* My dad may have exaggerated a touch about eating grass, but my cousin did tell me that the family was quite poor. When his own father began to earn money, he would often send some to his parents. They likely died as they lived, with little money but lots of hope. That was how he died too.

Dad would sit in an armchair, reading intently, oblivious to the noise of the houseful of his children playing the gramophone, or discussing events at school that day. He read the newspaper, the Readers Digest and the Catholic Digest. On starry nights he would sit on his camp-chair and recite the Rosary to himself. Then he would likely reminisce to himself about the trials of years gone by, the good friends that he knew, and the many cities he had lived in. His thoughts probably took him back to his early childhood when deprivation and despair shaped the man that he became. A good man. A person who valued his family far more than material things.

Another quotation he often mentioned was: 'True happiness is making other people happy'. He would become more articulate if friends visited, especially if there was a pint of rum hidden in the cupboard which he could share with them. Despite his meagre pension there was always a place at the dinner table for any visitors who came by in the evening. Good friends never called to say that they would visit. In those days people just showed up and were always given a hearty welcome.

I did not spend much time alone with Dad. However, sometimes he would take me shopping. We would find a tea shop after. I would eat an almond biscuit with my tea, while he sipped his cup and smoked his cigarette. I don't ever recall having any deep conversations with him. I was, after all, the second youngest in a pack of eight. Maybe he had done enough philosophizing to my elder siblings.

Perhaps I didn't know him as well as I should have, but just having him around was comforting. I am sure many children in those days felt as I did. Just having a parent around provided enough stability. The unseen bonds and the unspoken words are enough comfort for children.

I recall my father returning from shopping. His gait was distinctive, since he had pain in his joints. He often said to us: "Mind over matter". He did not want to visit a doctor, because he did not want to spend money on himself. Conserving money for the family was far more important. When Mum finally convinced him to go to our family doctor, Dad returned from his clinic without having seen him. The kindly doctor phoned us and mentioned that my father had waited ten minutes in his reception area and did not want to wait any longer and had left.

Regretfully his neglect of his health led to his early death at age sixty-eight. But then, he was a stoic man and never complained about aches and pains. I once went with him to view the treatment that he had for the pains in his legs. The holistic practitioner used a device that generated a small current in his body. I am sure it was not painless but after the treatment he told me he felt relieved of the pain. Most people would feel this way after the electric shocks end…

Another time he had a toothache but refused to go to a professional dentist. Instead he went to the marketplace where there were several Chinese entrepreneurs who practiced low cost dentistry. (Possibly the diplomas on their walls were in

Mandarin testifying that their skills were in Automotive Mechanics.) When he came home he discovered that the wrong tooth had been pulled! But no doubt, the price was a bargain...

Once a week, on Saturday evenings, he would play 'Housie' at one of the local public places. It was called Housie, because when you scratched out all numbers on the game sheet, you would yell "House!" Most of the time he would come back with a grim face, sometimes with a smile, if he had won a 'Line' which provided a small amount of money. If a 'House' was not called, the funds would be carried over to the following week to start building a 'Snowball'.

One evening he returned, with his usual grim face. He reached into his coat pocket and then flung all the rupee notes into the air. This may have been two thousand rupees which, at that time, would likely be the annual salary of most average wage earners. He had won the Snowball! Of course, he would ensure that this would be used for provisions, linen and necessary clothing for us children. His only reward may have been a pint of rum or a cup of sweet tea in the Irani cafe.

My father had booked a trip to visit his brother, Joe, in India. This would have been the only time that he spent money on himself for a vacation. Some days before he was to begin the trip, a telegram arrived. My brother Bert took the pink sheet of paper from the Post and Telegraph courier and glumly handed it to Dad.

It read: 'Hunting accident. Joe dead. Pray for his soul. Joyce.' I had never seen my father cry. This is what he did. "Five decades of the Rosary," he sobbed, "three completed. Two left." His sister, Dorothy (our Auntie Dot), and he, were the only siblings who remained.

In those days corporal punishment was the norm. We knew someone who punished his children very severely. My father was not like that. Mum would threaten us, when we were being naughty. "Your father will give you a good belting when he comes home." However, he would remove his belt and that was enough. He never struck us. We knew however, when he was angry with us. He would use the forbidden word 'damn'. We were all brought up with the absence of curse words at home and at school.

The British had realized that they had to give up India as a colony. As such, they decided to grant independence to his sub-continent. However, the Muslims, a minority in India, wanted their own country. 'Partition', the separation of the Dominion of India into two countries, India and Pakistan, finally took place. The break-up was a violent one. Blood-thirsty mobs of Hindus, Muslims and Sikhs, had been killing each other as Partition approached.

My father had believed that Christians would have a better future in Pakistan. We began our exodus in August 1947. Our train, the *Peshawar Express*, was one of the last trains to cross the border from India. Passengers on following trains to Pakistan or India, were slaughtered on both sides of the border. More than two million people were killed in the religious conflict that preceded, and followed, Partition. It is one of the most disturbing of past, and continual, chapters of our civilization that religion, which is supposed to ennoble followers, instead sometimes turns them into ruthless, violent pagans who massacre their own brothers and sisters.

I was told that our train had slowed as it approached the Pakistani border. I was an infant, the youngest of seven children in the family, at that time. My father and uncle closed all the blinds in the compartment looking out onto the platform. There were hundreds of bearded men with swords and knives who waited for the train to stop. Some Muslim families were pulled off the train and disemboweled on the spot. The door of our carriage was opened and the mob looked in. Two men on the platform entered our compartment with their knives drawn. Just then, one of the two men who had entered, recognized my father and said to his companion:

"Stop. He is a good man. He gave me money to visit my family in the village at the time my first child was born, when he was Telegraph Master in my town in India. I cannot forget that. Let them go to the promised land unharmed."

We were saved.

At the end of his life, he had been in a coma for two days. It was my turn to stand watch at his bedside in the Jinnah Central Hospital. That was the night when he moved on to a gentler place.

The man on the platform was right. He was a good man. He really was.

The following are some of the speeches that I have made to my Toastmaster's Club and other groups. The words capture, like an old photograph, my thoughts at that time of my life. Some details have been changed to protect the identity of persons and organizations who may wish to remain anonymous.

The Coral Beneath the Waves

Honoured guests, fellow members and especially our new members.

A few moments ago, you formally became part of a group which has a major impact on all aspects of society.

An association which has high standards and requires us to provide leadership and direction now, and as we approach the new millennium. An organization which, to ensure continuing excellence, has supported Continuing Professional Development knowing that, as B.F. Skinner said *'Education is what survives, when what has been learnt, has been forgotten'*.

So, I bid our new members a warm welcome to our profession.

Let me caution you however, that there is little glamour in this profession. Unlike television's lawyers, doctors, police officers and lifeguards, there is little drama in our work. You will never find yourself, or someone like me, in a lead role on *Baywatch*, although I have been asked many times…

We tend to keep a low profile in society. But this is critical and crucial to everyday living.

There are few aspects of my life which are not touched by one of our twenty-seven- thousand members. Gas, for my vintage 1986 Reliant Station Wagon, comes from a refinery which was designed and built by engineers. Heating for my home is a result of major discoveries of gas by our geologists and geophysicists. The food I eat is processed in machinery designed, built and operated in processing plants by our members.

And lest we forget, the important Sewage System is operated by our members in the City of Calgary Waterworks department. One of their consultants once told us that for twenty years, sewage had been his bread and butter...

So, if it is glamour you want, you have not chosen the right profession. But if you want to wake up your creativity, challenge your senses, and perhaps watch a piece of your creation land on Jupiter, or on the base of the Mariana Trench, welcome to our Association!

Many years ago, I gave up a very comfortable, secure job to study engineering at the University of Calgary. Four years later, I was at the Convocation at the Jubilee Auditorium. I still, very clearly, recall the stirring rendition of O Canada and the excitement I felt that I was soon to become an engineer.

Our country was brought together by risk-taking railroad engineers. Canadian geologists and geophysicists were continuing the pioneering spirit by searching for oil, gas and minerals in the jungles of Sumatra and in the icefields of Siberia.

I felt that I was soon to be part of this adventure: Indiana John...

My childhood dreams of designing and flying high speed aircraft, racing cars, etc. was perhaps about to come true. Well, not quite...

After graduation, I began my first job, expecting to become President of the corporation the following month. Although I did not make President, I can say that I have been extremely fortunate in working with a few, very exciting companies and many, many talented people over the last several years.

They have inspired me, coached me and constructively criticized me when I needed it. There were good times and trying times, but throughout my career, there was never any doubt that I had chosen the right Calling. And I am sure that most of you will feel the same way, many years from today.

Much like Eva, one of my three children, I enjoy opening fortune cookies. The messages are humorous and sometimes thought-provoking. My fortune cookie's message a few months ago was: *'May you always live in exciting times.'*

What, you may ask, is so exciting about this profession?

Why are there twenty-seven-thousand members still part of the Association?

How do we continue to attract the best and the brightest to our field?

It is because we work in a field which is changing, rapidly evolving and requiring us to continually adapt. The prerequisites of this profession are essentially: flexibility and adaptability.

'Adaptability' brings to mind the coral in the Great Barrier Reef. The reef stretches eighteen-hundred miles from New Guinea to Australia. Earl Nightingale, while on a guided tour of this fabulous reef, noticed that (in his own words) *'the coral polyps on the inside of the reef, where the sea is tranquil and quiet in the lagoon, appeared pale and lifeless... while the coral on the outside of the reef, subject to the surge of the tide and the power of the waves, were bright and vibrant, with splendid colours and flowing growth...'*

Earl asked the Guide why this was so.

"It's very simple," said the Guide, *"the coral on the lagoon side dies rapidly, with no challenge for growth and survival... while the coral facing the surge and power of the open sea, thrives and multiplies because it is challenged and tested, every day. And so it is with every living organism on earth."*

What you new members should learn from the colourful coral is to 'meet the challenges, adapt, grow and flourish.'

Changes have occurred within many organizations over the years and, within the last decade, it appears that the rate of change is increasing. It is true there has been restructuring of organizations which may be questionable, but there is little doubt that the opportunities for growth have increased due to the realization that new, exciting technologies require a highly educated, experienced and skilled workforce.

Alberta has, on a per capita basis, the highest educated workforce in the world. The opportunities for skilled, flexible, technical personnel have never been better. Industry Canada recently completed a study and determined that there are sixty-five-thousand persons employed in the Consulting field. This puts us in the top four on the world stage, in terms of revenues for Consulting. Our competitive advantages include Resource Extraction, Energy and Telecommunications.

To support this world leadership position, many companies in Canada have very aggressive recruitment programs to keep up with the high demand for skilled personnel. Our company get hundreds of resumes. The persons who get employed are those who demonstrate that they can be flexible, take risks and, most of all, that they can work effectively in a team.

The Pathfinder Mission to Mars was the result of such a team. To travel more than three hundred million miles and land a few miles off target, on a distant planet, is not one person's accomplishment, but an entire team of specialists. Each member has specific skills in specific areas. The team members must mingle, share ideas, meet the challenges, gain consensus and, only then, can project success be assured.

Nowadays, the team composition is different. Team members look different. They act differently, talk differently but, like the beauty of the coral, the end result is a mosaic which might have been the work by that great artist and scientist, Michelangelo.

Recently I was on a committee reviewing Diversity in the Workplace. Today's workplace sees different type of persons in key positions, where they were not present before. It sees diversity of cultures and genders in all positions in the workplace. This no longer surprises most Canadians who accept the skills and talents of various cultures and genders, much as they accept Hockey Night in Canada being distinctly Canadian.

Different cultures and genders bring a fresh, new perspective to the workplace. It enables corporations to better understand ways of doing business in other countries and has led to some very successful partnerships around the globe. Our company has been present in China since the seventies in a mutually beneficial partnership with a local company. Canadian companies have spearheaded work in Russia, India, Chile and Argentina. Putting our people on the world stage, competing with other countries, has required us all to think and act globally, and not to aspire to a lifetime job in downtown Calgary.

The first Star Wars movie which I saw some years ago, made an impression on me. It was not the high-tech action which left an impression. It was the scene at the bar. Yes, the scene at the bar...

What struck me about this scene was to see, fiction though it was, several aliens of different types, socializing in the same bar. I wondered, at the time, if something like this could ever be possible. A group of totally dissimilar beings, being in close proximity and socializing in apparent harmony.

I work in an environment today which has proved that it is not only possible, but is the assured way to success. There is value in diversity of opinions and perceptions. The diversity of language and the diversity of the way we think and act, has moved us forward. And the momentum is growing as we have seen in our industry. Rules are changing, routine does not exist anymore. The barriers have fallen and so has the Berlin Wall. The workplace is changing. For the better...

The tools we use today are better and are changing more often, more quickly and in more parts of the globe, than ever before in the technological age. As processing chips get faster, engines become more efficient, air quality gets better, you can applaud yourselves that you are part of an organization that has contributed to making life just a little bit better.

I am excited, and I am sure you are too, about the amazing potential there is for you to continue to work in a dynamic and challenging workforce. You are the leaders of today and tomorrow and will be required to keep up the impetus of these very positive times.

You have joined a group of friends who are dedicated to serving society by enhancing and providing leadership in the practice of your profession. I look to you inductees to continue our proud tradition of service to society, here in Alberta and around the globe. I sincerely wish you will always adapt to challenging events, like the coral beneath the waves.

Congratulations! Welcome to the Association.

APEGGA New Member Induction Ceremony
Calgary, September 1997

The Last of the Red-Hot Losers

'Tis better to have loved and lost, than never to have loved at all. So said Shakespeare, Ralph Klein, Wayne Gretzky, or somebody who was bright enough to coin the proverb. I have loved many in my short life and have lost most. Today I want to share my broken heart with you and explain why I am known to some as the Last of the Red-Hot Losers.

I was twenty-six years old, when my mother finally allowed me to go out on my first date. It was with a woman who had everything a man desired. Yes, Helga Hogan had it all. A strong back, broad shoulders and a big chest. She was not related to Hulk Hogan, but had recently won a look-alike contest (I assumed that was because they were both blonde.)

For entertainment we attended Stampede Wrestling, calf roping and watched reruns of King Kong and Godzilla movies. But our relationship couldn't last long. We were always fighting. And I was always losing. Finally, I escaped from her clutches (it was a Half-Nelson, if I remember correctly). I decided to search for someone more petite, someone whom I could arm-wrestle with, and win!

Voila! Into my life came Irma Latouche. She was the essence of all things feminine, delicate and wholesome. Her sweetness gave me a severe case of acne! Here I was twenty-eight years old with eruptions all over my face...but she was worth it. She was the princess I had dreamed about all my life. Our romance continued, through the spring, summer and fall. Ah yes, sunshine and roses and cute little giggles under the spreading poplars. My life was complete.

But alas! Twas under the August moon that she did decline to take our romance any further. After six months of courting, I dared to kiss her little cheek (under the spreading poplar) when she did strike my wanton lips, call me a beast and fly back to her mother...Mrs. Latouche.

I was shattered. I attempted suicide and jumped into the river. It had already frozen up, so I picked myself up from the ice and dragged my empty body home. I took to drinking. For many months I regularly drank up to twenty rounds of strawberry milkshakes at the local Dairy Queen, waiting for my cupcake to return. But she never did.

It was then that I began to go downhill (even though I preferred cross-country skiing). I let my hair grow to my shoulders, ceased to take showers, stopped using Old Spice and used garlic oil and onion juice instead. I started smoking grass. But the clippings tickled my nose. I then got into coke (Diet Coke, since I had to watch my weight).

Finally, I met Petunia, a young flower child. She was well connected. Her brother Percy, was the Vice President of a motorcycle gang, so I moved into the group. I started to wear dark glasses, imitation leather jackets dyed in pig swill, with bicycle chains for suspenders. The others had tattoos on their arms which said 'Mother', 'Father', 'Saskatchewan'. So I tattooed my biceps too, but I could only fit in the three-letter words like 'mum', 'dog' or 'cat'. (I was slightly underdeveloped). I began to carry a knife. And also a spoon and a fork.

I thought my little girl friend would le impressed but she soon tired of me and resented most of all that I still had a training wheel on my ten cc Honda. She was mad that I had to buy the type with a pedal start while all the others had the big Harleys. Needless to say, I was driven from the club in disgrace!

Here I was twenty-nine years old, with no woman in my life. What was I to do? So it was back to the river for another jump. It was frozen again, so I dragged myself to a nearby sewer for a good night's sleep.

The dawn broke and a new day began. "I must change." I said. "I must become a somebody. I must get married, buy a three-bedroom house, have three snotty-nosed kids and mow my lawn every Sunday. I must become <u>respectable</u>!"

So it was off to *K Mart*, to buy a good polyester suit and start my new life.

I met an archaeologist but she didn't dig me. I dated a farm girl, but she couldn't stand my bull. I even courted a Toastmaster, but she thought my gestures were obscene!

So here I am today, still searching for Ms. Right, or Ms. Left, or mistress. Searching the nightclubs, the sports clubs and searching my soul and crying out in the lonely night.

"Oh Lord, why me? Why am I the Chosen One? Why am I the Last of the Red-Hot Losers? What's wrong with that guy in Ottawa, whatshisname: 'Myron Baloney'?

April 1986

This speech won awards at a number of levels in the Toastmasters International contest. It was also my first experience in a Public Speaking competition. I surprised myself with the unexpected success.

Award Acceptance Speech

Thank you very much for inviting me today to recognize my company's successful twelve-year partnership with the High School. It continues to be as fresh and lovely as the dozen roses some of you received from your loved ones a few days ago, on Valentine's Day.

How does this Partnership benefit our own employees? What we see is youthful exuberance and enthusiasm. Something that may be missing in some organizations. If you want to be happy, be with happy people.

I have three children, only one of whom is still in school. Some years ago, I recall that Eva returned excitedly from kindergarten with a poster of the next day's event. The poster said 'Hurray, Hurray, it's Cupcake Day'. How could I not share her joy? Many of us do the eight-to-five routine and do not often revitalize ourselves with little happy events such as that was, for Eva.

In fact, on Valentine's Day, I had a happy event at the office. One of my co-workers walked into my office and asked if I'd like a kiss. Of course. She was handing out *Hershey's Kisses*. Now, didn't that make my day?! My wife was excited too when I rushed home and said "Hey, I got a kiss from an attractive lady at the office!"

Enthusiasm and high energy are key characteristics for employees of many successful companies. Our employees see this in the High School's artwork, drama and music productions.

Education today will, as always, continue to face a number of challenges. One of the challenges is the 'Promise of Technology'. All progressive organizations must incorporate technological advances on a continual basis. But these advances are made with a motivated workforce. If we did not have keen employees, we would soon perish as a business. We have a 'Passion to Build' as our current slogan. But our passion is not limited to building plants, manufacturing facilities, roads and bridges. Our passion is also to build better communities where we live and where we work.

How better to do this than to ensure that we will always have well-educated young leaders who will innovate and improve upon what we have done before?

Our young people will have this 'passion to build' in their lifetime and our vision is for them to be 'Master Builders of the Future'.

Our young people will see how walls do not divide. But instead, enclose and protect.

Our young people will build new roads to bring diverse communities closer together, to live in peace and harmony.

Our young people will build bonds among team players, which will serve as a model for successful organizations.

Our young people will continue to have tomorrow, the passion our founders had when they created the great infrastructure projects of yesterday and today.

The school and my company had humble beginnings in 1888. Our founder was a carpenter and at one time the school was nicknamed 'Sleepy Hollow High'.

Surviving for one-hundred years was not by chance. Instead, I believe we both survived and flourished because of the passion and resilience of our founders. Their passion lingered on, through all the generations that followed.

I thank you for recognizing or efforts to build better partnerships and communities and very much appreciate this award.

February 2004
This is an extract from an acceptance speech for an award to the company from the Calgary Board of Education.

Dying to Clothe You

Four hundred years ago, along the shores of the St. Lawrence River and Hudson's Bay, a very lucrative trade was being conducted. It was a trade that was instrumental in the birth of Canada. It was a trade built on necessity at that time.

I am referring to the Fur trade which has grown successfully over the years. Now our country ranks number three in the world behind the United States and the Soviet Union, in the supply of animal skins for fashion clothing.

These were the olden days when animal skins were one of the few alternatives we had to shelter us from the environment. These were essential articles of clothing at that time.

Nowadays, we have a variety of wools, wool blends and synthetic fibres that look good, feel good and are as effective as animal skins, in keeping us warm. We have matured and will continue to evolve and perhaps become more civilized so that we do not need to trap and slaughter small animals to satisfy the whims of the fashion designers in Paris.

Each year, millions of mink, beaver, fox, seal and other fur-bearing animals are savagely killed, poisoned and trapped for the sake of detestable dowagers who frequent the opera halls of Europe. The last record pelt production of modern times in Canada was in 1949 when ten million animals were killed in order to drape the backs of a vain multitude.

Last year, four million animals were brutally slain in Canada to protect the delicate skins of some superficial people as they emerged from their chauffeur-driven limousines and entered a concert hall to listen to music that they had little appreciation for.

Must these creatures be slaughtered for such an empty purpose?

Granted, we slaughter many more millions of animals for our tables. But this is somewhat different. We have developed habits in our diets over many generations for animal flesh. It was considered an important nutrient and a major source of protein and is eaten to sustain our lives. We cannot become vegetarians overnight, as there is not enough knowledge among the masses regarding the correct diet to follow.

But we should develop a sense of responsibility regarding the slaughter of animals purely for exotic clothing.

We have so much power on this earth but have misused it. We have wiped out the bison and the buffalo from the Great Plains. We still pursue animals in the wild, shoot them with arrows and bullets and then proudly mount their heads over our fireplaces and place their skins under our feet.

We needlessly torture several thousand animals in Research labs without considering the minimal value of some of this research. And now we continue to kill many millions of helpless animals so that we may use their precious fur for the sake of lifting our social status.

And after all this we call <u>ourselves</u> human beings and we call the animals: The Beasts!

Although we hear the sad stories of destroying the livelihood of the Trapper, the fact is that the Trapper makes approximately five hundred dollars a year from this part of the fur trade. Most of the money is made by the trading houses and the big designer houses in the industry.

Fifty years ago, the beaver almost became extinct due to the demand for beaver pelts. Today the wolverine and the lynx are close to extinction.

We do not need animal skins to keep us warm. We have alternatives. Furs are no longer essential items of clothing for the general population. I have never seen people in mink coats commuting to work or shopping at Safeway. These people only wear their exotic furs to attend a social event that demands the best from their closets. The furs are for the eyes only and not for the body.

We do not need to eradicate a species for the sake of fashion.

We do not need to satisfy the vanity of those socially backward people who buy skins as a status symbol and not for warmth.

If these superficial people could only see the lifeless, bulging eyes of hundreds of minks that had been suffocated...

If they could only see the brutal clubbing and the blood-spattered ice on our Atlantic shores...

If they could only see, and share the agony of an animal attempting to free itself from a leg-hold trap in the desolate forests of the north...

If they could only see all this, they would turn away in shame and grief and...they could perhaps feel in their hearts a sorrow for the creatures who have died for no other purpose than for Vanity.

I am not an activist for Animal causes. I am a mere citizen of the world who has been observing with sadness and guilt, the wanton acts of lust and violence we perpetrate on dumb animals, who were born to share this earth with us.

We owe them a living. We do not need to take their lives for naught. Their lives are as precious as our own. Like us, they have only one chance at living...

Why take it from them needlessly for an industry that belongs in our history books?

November 1987

A Paradox

'Tis strange how women kneel in church and pray to God above,
Confess small sins and chant and praise and sing that He is Love;
While coats of softly furred things upon their shoulders lie--
Of timid things, of tortured things, that "take so long to die"...
'Tis strange to hear the organ peal--"Have mercy on us, Lord",
The benediction -peace to all - they bow with one accord
While from the stained windows fall the lights on furs so softly warm,
Of timid things, of little things, that died in cold and storm...

1925, Edward Breck

Perhaps You have Lost Your Vision

Let me ask: How many of you would willingly move into a totally different type of job, at the same salary level, starting tomorrow morning?

I'm sure most of you, if you're like me, would hesitate to accept this because you are stepping into the unknown. You are stepping into unfamiliar territory. You suddenly have to re-educate yourself. You are back to zero. And you have to prove yourself, once again.

But there are many that have made major changes in their lives and have done quite well. There was a Pharmacist, at age forty-three, who said he was tired of reading doctor's prescriptions for the previous twenty years and decided to become a doctor himself. And he did it.

On a larger scale, Japan, which used to copy other country's products in the 1960s, decided to innovate, create and improve their quality so much that today they are world leaders in televisions, cameras, watches, cars and shipbuilding.

In our lifetime we have seen at least three major changes.

Political: the collapse of the East bloc.

Since 1950, the Soviet Union and their Allies were our worst enemy. In the West we accumulated a huge arsenal to combat the red peril of Communism.

I remember the time we came very close to a world war when the Soviet ships were heading for Cuba and John Kennedy sent his ships to confront them. That was a tense time. Today the threat is still there, but the likelihood of a war with the Soviet Union has been lessened considerably since their own country appears to be collapsing from within, after all their allies have abandoned Communism. A change in politics of this magnitude was not imaginable five years ago.

Workplace:

In the early fifties it was very unusual in the western world for women to hold any positions of responsibility in the working world. They were supposed to stay home, do the cooking and cleaning, and make sure that the children were well brought up, while Daddy brought home the bacon.

Today, a large chunk off the work force is made up of women, in professions that used to be dominated by men. These include: Medicine, Law and Engineering.

Personal:

Ten years ago, I got married just when I was a feeling so comfortable as a single man. Suddenly I was sharing the same home with somebody who didn't appreciate *Playboy* magazine. That was pretty serious. And she would argue with me. (I lost most of the arguments, I may add).

Finally, I got used to my dear wife and vice versa. But then, when a snotty-nosed kid arrived, it was chaos again. And later two more arrived, before I had recovered from the first one! Then they started to talk and argue and it was back to chaos. I go to the office now for rest and relaxation. Holidays. I hate them!

But through all these changes I've kept my sanity. Ask anyone here. They know me...

At my mature age, I even started learning the piano, before arthritis sets in. Who says piano is for kids only?

And let me remind you of a politician from Saskatoon by the name of Bob Ogle. Five years ago, his life saw a major change. He was diagnosed with a brain tumour, heart disease and a terminal blood disorder. While he was recovering from one of the treatment sessions his attending nurse asked him:

"What will you do when you get better?"

He replied that he didn't really know because he had done everything in his life. He had met Reagan, Gorbachev, Bush and had travelled to one hundred and twenty-three countries.

The nurse told him that she felt that he had lost his vision. Coincidentally, the next morning he became blind. He eventually recovered his eyesight but could never forget the words of the nurse 'perhaps you have lost your vision.' He has since accepted the change in his health and is ready for death.

When you come across what seems to be a major change in your life, see it as a challenge. Never lose sight of other goals in life. There will always be several changes in our lives and it is not necessary for us to consider any of these changes to be threatening. You can be sure of death and taxes but you may also be sure of change. Nothing ever remains the same. Weather changes, politics change, companies change, you change companies and so on.

Life really is made up of relentless changes. The challenge is to adapt to these changes with a minimum of stress and somehow survive. The fact that you are alive and well today and reasonably sane, proves that you can adapt to change.

If you do not have a few challenges in life your brain will atrophy. If you break your arm and don't use it for a period of time it will eventually wither away. Isn't it obvious that if you don't use your mental abilities the same will happen to you?

Do not be distressed by change. Look forward to it. It is one of the ways we will continue to stay sharp and alert. Do not look forward to a long and boring life. Look for things you can do today, after work, at home or at play, that offer you challenges. Change is essential for personal, business and national growth and is an abbreviated form of '**challenge**'.

Think about it, and many happy changes to you in your life.

June 1990

Swing Me Just a Little Bit Higher

Two thousand people lived in the city, but ten thousand came for the event. Ten thousand people waited in suspense for the two key players. They cheered loudly when they climbed the stairs to the stage. Another man stepped back, hit the lever, the trap-doors opened and the men fell twenty feet and broke their necks. And as their condemned souls rose from the pit of death, they looked down upon the cheering multitude. Yes, vengeance was immensely satisfying, to the people gathered in the city of Toronto in 1828...

There were other events in early Canadian history. A young boy, thirteen years old, was hanged for stealing a cow. Another young man for stealing a horse.

The dark side of our minds develops a morbid satisfaction when it comes to executions. The French Revolution saw housewives knitting at the guillotine, waiting all day for the ultimate in decadent enjoyment... the death of another human and the satisfaction of <u>being there</u>.

In 1861 hundreds gathered outside a Montreal prison to witness a double hanging. When one of the prisoners was pardoned at the last minute, the crowd was furious and a riot began. They stoned the police while the other prisoner was still swinging overhead.

These are our fellow human beings...

One hundred years later, several motorists stopped outside the Don Jail to be near the site of the last Canadian execution and to experience the thrill of <u>being there</u>.

These are our fellow human beings...

There was a woman in Hamburg, Germany, one of a crowd, who was waiting for a potential suicide to leap to his death. She complained that she had been waiting all morning and he still hadn't jumped!

Yes, these are our fellow human beings...

The primal urge to draw blood is still with us. The satisfaction in so doing, is euphoric.

Is it punishment we want? Or is it revenge?

Is it justice we want? Or is it entertainment?

Other lives are sacred no matter how despicable the person may seem. The State cannot play God, in that there is never absolute certainty of the guilt of others.

We create our own hell. There is more preoccupation with violence in North America, than in any other western nation. We are thrilled by the macho action on television. We clap with lust at the gratuitous violence in the movie, *Rambo*.

We applaud the tough hockey player who sends his opponent crashing into the boards. How many of us know that forty-two young hockey players have suffered spinal chord injuries during the years of 1976 to 1983? Seventeen are totally paralyzed. But the game must go on, and the team owners must reap their profits over the broken bones of our young children.

Thousands scream for the right to possess handguns. Millions of Canadians cheered when a man shot a robber in the back, in cold blood. Few read the letter from the robber's mother in the newspaper, telling us that there are some children in this world who do indeed, go astray.

Yes, thousands across Canada contributed to the shooter's defence fund. But none would consider consoling the helpless mother of that petty thief, as she grieved in the dust, by his grave.

And in this turmoil of a world gone mad with revenge, the chorus rises for the return of Capital Punishment.

How many lethal injections and broken necks must there be before we have drunk our fill from the Cup of Vengeance?

Why won't we accept that, regardless of the death penalty, the statistics will be unchanged?

In any population there will always be some that have the propensity for violence. And, if the conditions are right, the crime will be committed.

It has been proven time and again that Capital Punishment is not a deterrent. The Police Associations know that and so do many social psychologists.

Why do we want to raise the spectre again?

Killing these few will not change the numbers. In fact, in '75, before the abolition of Capital Punishment, there were 3.09 homicides per 100,000. After abolition, the latest figures available is 2.78 per 100,000. A drop.

So why do we want to reinstate it?

Instead of dealing with the other major problems in this country such as unemployment, deficits, trade wars, etc., our politicians decide to distract the population with an emotional issue such as Capital Punishment. Every politician in Alberta (except Joe Clark) supports the return of the noose.

Why do Europe and Japan have far fewer murders that the USA? They don't have Capital Punishment.

Many approve of selective Capital Punishment. 'In certain cases,' they say. The murderer of a policeman? Why not the rapist, the terrorist, the child molester and the bank robber? Why not the tramp on the street who is draining our tax dollars?

Where will it end?

We still want the spectacle. We still want the blood. We still want the state sanctioned entertainment of the brutal killing of our fellow man.

Have we really advanced?

There is some question in my mind about whether I would sanction the killing of someone who has killed a loved one. But that would be revenge. An immediate reaction of someone who has lost a loved one. And that is wrong.

How many of us would ask for the hanging of the shooter of the petty thief? It was murder, after all. Shooting an unemployed thief in the back was not an accident. But no, he is a folk hero, because he was protecting his property, which to some of us is far more sacred than a human life.

Few realize that the ones who are executed are the 'losers' who don't have a good lawyer. We use these miserable wretches as our human sacrifice to appease our conscience for what is wrong in our society.

The criminals who are responsible for the deaths of thousands are far too wealthy to be executed, or they are politicians who are far to famous to pay the ultimate sacrifice.

Can you recall one Mafia Don ever being executed? No, they are special people. They have money and power. The noose is only for the socially disadvantaged, the scum of the earth, those creatures who dwell in the torment of severe mental disorders, for whom no tears would be shed...

We have progressed immensely since the dawn of man. We have conquered plague and small pox. We have conceived the most beautiful music and songs. We have conquered the mountains and oceans and have touched the moon.

We have done so much...and have come so far.

Let's not go back...

March 1987

A Case for Compassion

Some years ago, I had a bad dream. I dreamt that I was lying alone on the street and slowly dying without anybody around to comfort me. I felt that, at moments near death, most people would like someone near them to help them along. But this is not really that bad compared to some of the daily tragedies that many are suffering today.

There are many who are near death who are not only dying alone, but are being abandoned by family and friends. I speak of the victims of acquired immunity deficiency syndrome: AIDS. A disease for which there is no known cure. The disease that is killing several thousand people around the world. In some countries it is killing many people but figures are being suppressed by these countries to keep the tourists coming.

The highest risk group in North America is the gay community and herein lies the problem. In our North American society, a person with AIDS is immediately branded a homosexual and with that comes the ridicule and humiliation. These victims leave this world with all the hate and loathing heaped on them by thousands of sanctimonious individuals.

There is the case of Michael K. Michael was the son of Jane and David. On July 11, 1987 he was diagnosed as having AIDS. In the latter stages of the disease he developed Cryptococcosis which makes people crazy. He once pulled his intravenous line and ran down the steps of the Foothills Hospital in a mad frenzy. When he suffered convulsions and seizures with his high temperature, his father was there to hold him. At the height of his hallucinations his mother was there beside him. He was one of the 'lucky ones'. Michael died within five months and in that time not a single family member or friend rejected him.

Many AIDS victims develop other debilitating ailments and suffer for many months or years before they eventually die. There was the case of a young child who developed AIDS through a blood transfusion. The entire community in a small town in the U.S. wanted him out of the school. There was someone who once told me that they shouldn't search for a cure for AIDS because it would get rid of all the homosexuals. Another person tried to commit suicide since he belonged to a well-known, religious family and had to hide his inclination from them. Fortunately, he was assisted by a support group and continued to live a happy and productive life with family and friends. He had tried hard to change his inclination so that he would be accepted by society but was unable to do so. He was born that way and did not become gay as some people believe.

If someone is born a homosexual is it right for us to wish that he dies of AIDS? I am suggesting that we should accept that there are many amongst us who are not as fortunate as we are. When they fall ill, we must not preach to them that the wrath of God has befallen them, and that they deserve the misery that they are going through. They deserve the understanding and compassion that is due to them. They are still our brothers and sisters who need care and attention like any other terminally ill people.

There isn't a religion in the world that does not promote Compassion and there isn't a single person on this earth who would not be considered a Sinner by someone else. Hence, I find it difficult when some people tell me that people are suffering because they deserve to.

Although AIDS appears to be confined to the gay community, it is not limited to this group. The disease has been transmitted to heterosexuals too, and these will also be subjected to contempt by some ignorant people.

In the Middle Ages they used to beat people with epilepsy because they thought that they were possessed by the devil. People with leprosy are still shunned today even though it is the least contagious of diseases. Victims of Lou Gehrig's disease are ridiculed by many.

Through the centuries we really haven't changed and in these modern times AIDS is as terrifying as the Bubonic Plague was a few centuries ago. Victims of this disease suffer considerable physical and psychological pain due to the ignorance of the masses. The ugliness of the disease is not the disease itself. But the ugliness is the reaction to this disease by the sanctimonious.

If we care about humanity, if we care about the disadvantaged and if we care about the victims of AIDS, the greatest gift to them will be compassion and understanding and hopefully, sometime in the future, they will leave this world in a happier frame of mind.

March 1989

Three Blind Mice

As we sit here today we are being robbed. We are being robbed by many unseen criminals in positions of influence. Wealth and riches are what many have desired over their lifetime and, believe it or not, some have succeeded. Yes, let me tell you about three individuals whose quest for power was successful. I call them the three blind mice because they were so blinded by their greed.

Let me tell you first about Ferdinand Marcos. He is worth about ten billion dollars today, while his country owes that much for its national debt. He stole ten billion dollars from his people. His followers and countrymen were living in appalling conditions, yet he plundered his country's treasury.

But then, he was ambitious.

Martin was a key man on Wall Street whom some of you may have heard of. He was recently convicted of grand larceny for using inside information to line his pockets with many millions of dollars. Last November he agreed to pay a penalty of one hundred million dollars for a swindle in which he had profited to the tune of fifty million. He once lectured some undergraduates at a Business school and maintained that Greed was Good! He cheated others to amass his fortune.

But then, he too, was ambitious.

Closer to home we have Peter, who was a professional person with excellent credentials. This man stole two million three hundred thousand dollars from his client's Trust funds. He was convicted in 1981 to ten years in prison. However, today he is a free man since he was a model prisoner.

But then, he too, was ambitious.

These three men were so blinded by their ambitions that they were unable to stop their excesses until they degenerated into gluttony. One billion dollars stolen from his countrymen was not enough for Marcos. One hundred million dollars was not enough for Martin. Peter's grimy hands even grabbed his mother's money.

You may, like I do, find it difficult to visualize ten billion dollars other than knowing its a whole pile of money. If Marcos plundered his country's treasury for ten billion, he had stolen the average annual wage of over five million Filipinos. He, and several generations of his family and cronies, could never spend all that money in their lifetimes. Such was the magnitude of his greed.

When I think of these men I also picture Oliver Twist in an orphanage, holding up his empty bowl and asking: "Please sir, can I have more?"

When I think of these men I also picture one hundred thousand African children with bloated bellies, brutalized by their greedy leaders.

I think of these things and I ask myself: "Why do so few, have so much? Is wealth attained through hard work, as I was so often taught, or is it through cheating your fellow man?"

When does ambition end, and greed begin?

I am guilty, as so many of us are, of ambition. Today I have a lot more than I had last year. But am I happier with my additional material assets? It is arguable. The quest for self - sufficiency can easily turn into greed. We never have enough. We all want more, and more, and more, and others want much more.

What I find so appalling is that there are so many in public life, whether it be in professions, politics, rock groups, television evangelists, whatever, who many look up to as examples of success. These ambitious, greedy, insensitive and selfish people care so little about the example they set for their children, our children and many of their followers. Morals and ethics are thrown to the wind as these degenerates set about their goals.

While others are hungry, these eat caviar. While others are homeless, these own hundreds of acres of plush land dotted with mansions. While others are dying in their service, these trample their bodies to grab their property.

I ask you, are these men of success, or are they scavengers of society? There have been many more in history who have gone done this road and there will be many more. But wait... how much land does a man need?

The answer is six feet by four feet by ten feet deep. In the end we all have the same. In the end we all have a handful of soil thrown after us by the living, thrown in love, or thrown is disgust.

The choice is ours...

May 1987

Paul's Roast

I am a man of the cloth and have served my flock for many years. 'Brother John' they call me. My specialty is Exorcisms.

I was given a mission from the Vatican. And Head Office. A devil existed within our offices and my mission was to find him and get him out...

My search began in Head Office and then in our London and other European offices, until I landed in Calgary. I felt his presence at this location. He was here! For two years my quest continued. Finally, on October 31, just before the sun set, I looked at the office phone directory and saw the numbers '666'. The mark of the Devil. To mislead others a number '1' preceded these numbers. But I was not fooled. I knew that my long search had ended. I had found him!

With trembling fingers, I dialed the extension 1666. Shivers ran up and down my spine as the phone rang, six times, before it was answered... "Paul" the Creature answered. Nonchalantly. But I knew it was the Prince from Hades...

I went down to his office in the basement (as expected), close to the Furnace Room. The office reeked of sulphurous vapours. There was also the faint smell of Trident gum, which he chewed hungrily while his eyes gleamed like burning coals.

He was smoking a cigarette. He blew rings at me and gave me an evil smile. This did not deter me from entering this den of iniquity. His black cloak was hung behind his door. His cloven hooves were hidden by a pair of cheap boots bought at the local *K Mart* store. This had to be Satan. I was sure I was not mistaken.

I was disguised as an Engineer, complete with slide rule in my plastic pocket, prominent buck-teeth and ears that put the bats wings to shame. He was masquerading as a Buyer. It was the classic battle of Good versus Evil.

His co-workers told me that everywhere he walked, the animals would become skittish. Catty people would arch their backs and shriek. German (the Shepherds in our flock) would howl. Asses bared their teeth. Sheepish people would go 'Bah Bah'. They said that he was often outside the office front door, meeting with strange people, all of them enveloped in a cloud of white smoke. It was definitely not Philip Morris, Winston or Kent...any one of them could break a Camel's back.

His power was intimidating, but I would rise to the challenge. I had to. There was nobody else. I had searched for religious secretaries but there were none. They had all lost their innocence to some monster...

I tried to spike his drink with Holy Water, but it had no effect. Prayer meetings did not work either (we got no new Contracts). Candles lit and placed outside his office door sputtered and flickered out.

One evening, when I was driving home, I heard a voice. It said: 'Your windshield washer is low'. But then the clouds parted and I came to a screeching halt. Another voice in my brain, said: 'The solution is in the future.' And then it dawned on me what needed to be done. A remote office in the hot desert was working on the Project of the Future. And there was where Paul was banished to! We finally got rid of the Devil.

January 1994

Where is the Eagle?

Did you look in your garbage can this morning? I did, and found: two milk cartons, one can of dog food, one can of cat food, one ketchup bottle, five diapers, some spaghetti, eggshells and teabags.

Looking in my garbage can is not my favourite pastime, but I am a typical North American who dumps more waste into a garbage bag than any other person in the world. The average Canadian household throws out two thousand pounds of garbage per year. This works out to more than one hundred and sixty pounds per month for the average family. Americans dispose of sixteen billion diapers, two billion razors and two hundred and twenty million tires per year.

Considering the average good quality diaper takes about four hundred years to disintegrate, it could be said that we will be 'Pampering' many future generations. I'm sure they would not want us to pamper them so much.

Last summer, fifty miles of prime American beaches from New York City to Long Island were inundated with hospital waste and were closed to swimmers.

All this is stunning, but our lifestyles continue unchanged and we still throw out several pounds of material every day.

With the invention of Styrofoam, North Americans became the 'disposable society'. Styrofoam coffee cups, Styrofoam containers for your Big Mac, Styrofoam containers for eggs, meat products, and so on and so on, the list is endless.

Styrofoam was a remarkable invention years ago. It was light, could be moulded into various attractive shapes and it retained heat and cold. But little did the inventors realize that several tons of Styrofoam would outlast them by hundreds of years and travel across the oceans and remain virtually intact.

I recall the *Man from Glad* telling us that *Glad* garbage bags were the strong ones. They are. They are made of a thicker material than the other brands and can hold more weight. But therein lies the problem. The bag seals the contents well. It takes several generations before the bag disintegrates, since it is not biodegradable. The *Man from Glad* will no longer be wearing his white suit, but years from now, all that will remain will be his skeleton holding the bag...

We have adapted to the routine of having our garbage hauled away every week and taken out of sight and out of smell. Little do we realize that this waste goes to a landfill site, or to an incinerator, and does not just vanish into thin air.

Landfill sites require several acres of valuable land. In Alberta we have been told that we presently have sufficient landfill sites up to the end of this century. But consider the city of Toronto. The Keele Valley landfill site (just north of Toronto) was opened only five years ago and was supposed to last until the year 2000. It is now estimated to be filled within the next two years!

Finding another landfill site raises the 'Nimby Syndrome': Not In My Back Yard. Everyone wants to dispose of their garbage but they don't want the site within smelling distance. Landfill sites have proven to be a major problem for heavily populated countries. West Germany has deemed that thirty-eight to fifty-thousand landfill sites are potentially hazardous to the groundwater supply. None of these sites were sealed from the environment. Millions of tons of waste leach through the earth and find their way into groundwater, rivers and lakes. Three million tons of hazardous waste has been exported to Africa and Eastern Europe by North America and Western Europe. Landfill sites will not be as available anymore since current knowledge has proved them to be an environmental time bomb. Moreover, most residents won't want them to be too close to their homes.

Incineration was thought to be a good solution but has generated controversy due to the emissions from the stacks. Heavy metals, sulphur dioxide, nitrous oxides, arsenic and other hazardous materials are emitted during incomplete incineration. Ash produced after incineration is considered to be a highly concentrated pollutant containing dioxins that have to be dumped somewhere. The form of dioxin 2,3,7,8-tcdd is a very toxic molecule. No safe level of exposure to this is known, similar to plutonium.

A cargo ship named *The Pelicano* left Philadelphia in 1986 with a cargo of fourteen-thousand pounds of toxic incinerator ash and sailed the seas for two years looking for a country that would accept the garbage. The captain finally dumped four-thousand pounds of incinerator ash off the coast of Haiti. The balance was believed to be dumped somewhere on the high seas.

The city of Windsor, Ontario, has hotly contested the construction of an incinerator in the city of Detroit since the stack emissions are spread over their city. Incineration technology is still progressing but it is not at a pace that can keep up with our rate of garbage disposal.

It is interesting to note the parallel with nuclear waste. One of the major problems facing the nuclear industry was the disposal of several tons of radioactive waste from power plants. Many tons of waste are presently in so called 'safe storage', but presently this waste is sufficient to resurface the entire Trans Canada highway.

Our factories waste substantial amounts in their production processes. The 3M company recycled and reused some of their material and saved $320 million last year. A chemical company in Holland decreased their waste by ninety five percent by adopting a new process.

The problem of Waste is a major one for all of us on this earth. If any of you have ever owned an aquarium you can appreciate the problem. The aquarium is virtually a closed system. The fish exist happily in their ten or fifteen-gallon tank, and if they are really happy, they will reproduce. Food is given to the fish, some of it is eaten, some is wasted and deteriorates in the tank. Some of it passes through the bowels of the fish. If this waste is not removed by regular cleaning, the aquarium eventually becomes a toxic soup. The fish die in advance of this happening. The Earth is similar, except that our waste has nowhere to go. Burying it creates problems, and burning it creates other problems.

What remains to be done? The problem must be attacked at the source. The source is you and me. Let's consider what you and I could do first. Here are just a few suggestions:

Recycle our newspapers. There are many depots that accept newspapers. Take them there, or collect them for a group, such as the Boy Scouts, to pick up. A ton of paper requires three-thousand-seven-hundred trees and two-thousand-four hundred gallons of water. Why not recycle paper?

In the office: Ask for a box of 8x10 computer paper instead of 11x17. Print only the material that needs to be printed and copy only the minimum number.

Ask for paper instead of plastic bags at the grocery store. The paper bags are sometimes made of recycled paper and disintegrate much faster than plastic ones.

Minimize purchase of products in the grocery store that have metal packaging. Tomato juice is available in paper and metal cans. Buy the paper carton. It is interesting to note that in Europe most of the food products have only paper packaging and not metal. This makes separation and disposal much easier.

Don't throw out appliances that need minor repair. A friend of mine was surprised that I bought a gasket to repair my leaky dishwasher instead of throwing it out and buying a new one.

Don't buy unnecessary appliances such as an electric can opener. This has always been a 'cutting reminder' to me of the classical non-essential item. Electric can openers are fine if you are opening ten cans at a time, but when you open one a day, this could be done manually and is a great way for some of us to get our daily exercise...

Another 'non-invention' was the disposable camera by Kodak. Thank goodness it never caught on.

Crush cartons, such as milk cartons, before you throw it into the garbage. The garbage truck does compact it to some extent but you can assist in reducing the volume of garbage you have.

You don't need to change your car antifreeze every year despite what the service station tells you. Some service stations dump the antifreeze into the sewer and this ends up in our groundwater and rivers. One teaspoon of antifreeze causes irreversible kidney damage which results in death shortly thereafter.

Reduce the amount of plastic you buy that is disposable. In the 60's many of us thought plastics were a wonderful product since they do not deteriorate. Unfortunately, we have found them to show up generations later, on remote islands in the Pacific, virtually intact, even though they were dumped into the oceans and were exposed to the elements for many years. Many dolphins, whales and sea lions die each year after ingesting floating plastics or getting ensnared in plastic fishing nets.

Never did the people who developed plastics think that this would come back to haunt them. This is the price of progress.

Many of you can come up with your own solutions, since only you know what you throw out. Trudeau said the state has no right in the bedrooms of the nation, but the state will soon have a big say in what you have in your garbage can.

We are learning from other crowded cities how to cope with this problem. In the city of West Berlin, households have to pay for each garbage can they rent from the city. If you want additional garbage cans you must lease it. If you put out additional items, or two garbage cans, these will not be taken away, and you will be fined. Disposal sites for glass are within walking distance in most neighbourhoods and you may not throw away glass in the garbage.

Japan recycles approximately fifty percent of their waste, Western Europe thirty percent and the United States a meagre ten percent.

Our schools must highlight the waste disposal problem we have, and educate children as to the potential hazards of a lifestyle that encourages the production of waste. Manufacturers must develop alternative packaging to their products.

Our environment is similar to that of the fish in my aquarium. The difference is that each of us has the power to change our environment, and each of us must increase our education and awareness of this major problem facing us. Each of us has the responsibility of leaving the Earth with a rich heritage rather than a mountain of garbage.

As the putrefying odours from hundreds of thousands of landfill sites fill our nostrils, we may recall some of the words of an Indian chief of the Duwamish tribe who wrote to a US president in 1855 the following:

'The whites too, shall pass perhaps sooner than the other tribes. Continue to contaminate your bed and you will one night suffocate in your own waste. When the buffalo are all slaughtered, the wild horses all tamed, the secret corners of the forest heavy with the scent of many men, and the view of the ripe hills blotted by talking wires. Where is the thicket? Where is the eagle? Gone....'

February 1989

A Cloud on Our Horizon

We have, throughout history been aggressive to our fellow man and will continue to be so in future. The rocks and clubs have now evolved into nuclear weapons which, when used, will wreak far more destruction than this earth has ever seen. It is ironical that all countries have a Ministry of Defence but none have a Ministry of Offence, and that every war that has ever been waged, has been waged for purely 'defensive purposes'. Knowing that we will inevitably enter another major dispute in the years ahead because we have historically done so, is now a major concern. It is a concern and a fear because of the widespread loss of life on an immediate basis and also on a long-term basis. We may survive the initial onslaught but will probably die later due to radiation sickness or by famine.

Many do not realize how fragile our civilization is. North Americans felt that a nuclear war would occur in Europe and not involve us at all, so all would be well after the bombs had been exchanged. Due to the recent accident in Chernobyl, some of us have been startled to find radioactivity in drinking water in Edmonton, thousands of miles away from the disaster. Vast areas of farmland in the Soviet Union are now uninhabitable due to fallout. So, should a nuclear war take place, there will be a substantial impact on food and water in many areas of the world. Survivors will be competing with each other for the limited amount of food and water available and further continue the battle for survival.

The war cannot be won, but the danger is that many believe it can be won by nuclear means, and therein lies the problem. An accidental start of a nuclear war is a very real possibility, since no matter how carefully a system is designed, there will always be something that could go wrong. It could be an instrumentation error, or human error. A terrorist well educated in nuclear weapons, or a smaller country with access to nuclear weapons, can do far more destruction than was previously possible.

What can we do to forestall this? The first thing is to have a firm belief that you most certainly will die, or have a major change in your lifestyle, which you may not be able to adapt to. Although some survivalists have a year's supply of food in their basements, they don't realize that living in a totally enclosed space will not be possible for an extended period of time without a negative effect on their mental abilities. They will still have to breathe air that is contaminated and they will eventually develop cancer.

Secondly, we should encourage our leaders not to start or support any form of aggression, whether it be done by ourselves or by our allies.

Thirdly, we should try to educate ourselves and our children about the dangers of radiation.

Lastly, try to keep in touch with organizations that attempt to prevent nuclear war. All of them are not communist kooks who are trying to undermine our system. We owe our children the right to live on this earth just as we have.

September 1986

J.G. Barrie

A Minute in the Life of Napoleon

We have heard of the conquests and the military prowess of Napoleon and Caesar. We have seen the artistry of Van Gogh and have enjoyed the works of Dostoevsky. We have accepted them, but we have not accepted sixteen thousand people in this city, who, like them, have epilepsy.

Epilepsy, to most of us, is an unbearable condition for which there is no cure. Victims suffer severe discrimination due to our lack of understanding of the condition. Some even believe it to be contagious. In fact, when I was a young boy, I happened to witness someone having a seizure. My parents told me to stand back, since contact with his saliva would make me get the condition too.

The fact is that it is as contagious as a broken leg and does not impair the mental abilities of its victims as Julius Caesar, Dostoevsky and Bonaparte have proved.

It usually afflicts children and young people in the age group of three to twenty years. There are also cases where adults in their thirties contract it, but that is quite unusual. Normally it is the toddler to teenager group that get this condition.

Epilepsy is not a disease in itself but is merely a symptom of many different diseases that result in recurrent convulsions. These disorders may be a brain tumour, a brain malformation, head injury or encephalitis. In ninety percent of the cases the cause is not diagnosed. The seizure process is caused by uncontrolled electrical activity in the brain.

There are two main types of seizures: the most well-known type is classified as the 'grand mal' seizure. It is also the most terrifying one for a parent who is an onlooker. A grand mal seizure is very abrupt. The victim may become pale, pupils may dilate, the eyeballs roll upward, the face will distort and the person will fall to the ground and have severe muscular spasms for thirty seconds to three minutes.

Although this is a terrible sight, the victim is not suffering during the seizure, and is merely responding to confused messages from the brain. People who have lived long with this condition and are on medication, usually have only one or two seizures per year. It is not a daily event.

What can you do to help, if you are a witness to a seizure? The thing to do in this situation is to keep the area around the person free, so that he does not hurt himself, and wait until the convulsions end. Do not leave him alone. Keep him on his side so that he does not choke on his saliva. Do not put anything in his mouth. The myth about holding his tongue so that he does not choke is an old wives' tale. If the convulsions last more than ten minutes call an ambulance.

The other common type of seizure is called the "petit mal" or "absence" type. Children usually are seen to have staring spells, rolling of the eyeballs, nodding of the head or slight muscular movements. During these periods, patients lose consciousness for no more than thirty seconds. This is a problem for school-going children as they lose their ability to concentrate and are mistakenly believed to be backward. Most parents are unaware of the problem and most family physicians are not able to diagnose this type.

There are presently upwards of six hundred active cases of juvenile epilepsy being treated in the Children's Hospital in Calgary. In over ninety percent of the cases the causes are unknown. A big problem for the person with epilepsy is the social ramifications. We have a condition that is not life-threatening other than the person attempting suicide due to his or her inability to be accepted by their peers or to be accepted for employment. It grieves me that there are sixteen thousand people in this city who fear a job interview or a date. There are sixteen thousand people who wish to apologize for their condition. There are sixteen thousand people out there who need our understanding and acceptance.

Let's give them a chance...

December, 1987

Heroes of the Human Spirit

I speak today not of the heroes that are immortalized in the pages of our history books. I do not intend to praise the conquests of Julius Caesar, Alexander the Great and Napoleon Bonaparte. Instead, I wish to speak of the heroes of the human spirit, who are known to some of us, but not to all. You will not find my champions in the chronicles of the future, or the encyclopaedias of the present. Nor are they enshrined in the impeccable prose of the great novelists. Their tombs will not be visited by multitudes, instead they will probably be forgotten in the decades ahead.

One of whom I speak is Rick Hansen, who began his twenty-five-thousand-mile journey eighteen months ago, without all the fanfare and adoring crowds that accompany the sports idols of today.

Handicapped by a car accident at age fifteen, he did not lose his courage and resolve. He did not lose his spirit of survival like many of us who, perhaps, would have submitted to our abject condition and thereafter wallowed in self-pity.

He began an incredible voyage through thirty-three countries, along the highways and alleys and streets and valleys, through the rain, the frost, the cold and the heat, the snows and the winds, to prove his indomitable spirit could not be contained by his handicap.

Another champion of mine and a friend of Rick Hansen's, was Terry Fox, who refused to give up, and limped past the limits of human endurance, into our hearts and into the heavens.

Steve Fonyo is another courageous man, who has made some mistakes as a youth, since he is human, like all my heroes. But the joy he felt when he set his foot in the ocean, was a joy that we all felt simultaneously.

What makes these men so outstanding is that they chose to fight their disability, rather than succumb to a lifetime of anguish. They have increased our awareness of thousands of less fortunate people, who are afflicted physically and mentally.

It is shocking that it is our ignorance of the disabled that forced Terry Fox onto the desolate highways. We killed him! It is our patronage and condescending attitude that forces men such as these to commit these heroic acts. We close our minds to the handicapped and expect them to be institutionalized when many of them can be productive citizens in the mainstream of society. We seldom see a disabled person in our workplaces, instead we strip them of their pride and commit them to a purgatory of condescension and handouts. Our social attitudes are such that if I were to be disabled tomorrow, I would immediately be given financial support and forever be relegated to the backwoods of daily living. For me to work again would be totally incomprehensible in our system.

It is difficult, if not impossible, for the handicapped to pursue a normal career. The daily routine of life is geared to the so called healthy ones. How many more miles does Rick

Hansen's wheelchair have to roll, before we realize that he is as good, or better, than you or me?

I was moved many years ago, when I witnessed a victim of cerebral palsy who was being interviewed on television. She spoke of her desires for a lover, like many normal single people would. It moved me because, in my immense ignorance, I had never considered that people so severely afflicted would have feelings and desires just like you or me.

The disabled need our friendship, support and understanding, not necessarily our money or our platitudes. Our appreciation of their capabilities is far more important than our generous monetary offerings. They are equal, or better than we are, in some respects. All they want is a chance to lead a productive life in dignity. The disabled are helpless because we have branded them such. They are fragile, because we have convinced them that they are. Until recently our cruel language called them 'cripples' but now, in our benevolence, we call them 'disabled'.

To clear up these misconceptions, Fox, Fonyo and Hansen must make their painful journeys across our inhospitable lands, when they would much rather be working by our side, like so called 'normal' human beings.

There are countless other unsung heroes who are quietly struggling for survival and recognition. They fight valiantly against our prejudices and expect no praise, but only our understanding. Each dawn heralds another battle and each sunset lengthens the shadows of their grief and despair. They live with hope and passion in their hearts. Passion to partake in all the activities that we allow them, and hope that we will appreciate them as our peers. They need our recognition of their abilities and talents. We must not force them into formidable marathons in order to prove their equality.

These champions of whom I have spoken, have had their trials, but have been strengthened and have emerged from their crucible of torment, glowing with a moral light that will forever cheat the darkness of despair.

Think of them as your equals, for that is what they are. Let them share your labours and give them back their dignity and pride.

For they are the champions. And they are the heroes of the human spirit.

November 1986

Doug's Roast

I am shocked and disappointed that others would make light of my hero, Doug. From the moment I saw him seven years ago, skulking through the corridors of our office in a white coat and carrying sample bottles in both hands, I knew that he was someone special.

I then began to research his past career and his many accomplishments. His employment started with a bang when he found a job as an Explosives Detonator. He left no stone unturned as he blasted his way through the hills of Quebec, creating highways where no man had dared to go before: a one-hundred and thirty-decibel boom here, and a boom-boom there, and then he would head for the bars to rendezvous with Fifi Latouche. He was a hit with Fifi because he blew her mind, even though he had a short fuse. Fifi, who now teaches Nuclear Physics at Laval University told me that until she met Doug, she had not believed in the Big Bang theory.

What followed him later was a horde of flies, not because of the condition of his underwear, but because he studied Entomology. He studied mosquitoes, cockroaches and even slept with bedbugs in his pickup, just because of his enthusiasm for his work. An Ant finally found another, more sophisticated field of research for Doug, and that was when he got involved in the Clean Air Act and sprayed copious quantities of *Lysol* onto his underwear.

His later endeavor was to recover silver from film in a Crime Lab while stationed in Ottawa. This project lasted several months. He worked furiously in the dark room amidst fizzing, bubbling liquids, ten-gallon drums of ethyl alcohol, and several female undercover agents. At the end of the project he emerged from the dark looking tired and run-down, but yet immensely satisfied. The undercover agents also looked fairly satisfied and there were streaks of silver in their golden hair. Yes, since that time he has been known as the silver-tongued devil of the police, and also the original Silver Fox.

One of his well-known studies while he was working elsewhere, was to plot the magnetic field in the vicinity of Vancouver Island and also to measure acid rain accumulations. What would you say to a man who was walking along the beach with a compass in one hand and a tin mug in the other? It takes guts to embark on such a study, especially when you are being followed by a team of beach-bums shaking their heads.

Our Doug had courage, strength and resolve to embark on such an expedition. It did not matter that he was heading south on the island looking for the north pole! It did not matter that he was slightly off course (by a few thousand miles)! It did not matter that a horde of seagulls attacked him and took away his compass, thereby ending his expedition! Doug should be proud of that study. Every Salt who runs aground in the Inside Passage has two words to say to Doug.

His other opportunity arose when he was to head up a team to handle Solid Waste Management. One of his team members, Stinky Lapoo (also from La Belle Provence), has the highest regard for him and told me that he was knee deep in solid waste and always shoveling.

I have learned a lot from Doug. Before I met him, I thought David Suzuki was a motorbike. He cares about sour gas emissions! He has not developed a sour disposition and does not emit gas occasionally despite what his colleagues say. He cares about noise pollution and now works with the noisiest person in the office to try to rehabilitate him.

He has often been seen in the ditch along the highway picking up pop bottles and cans and has been seen in the back alley of the Cecil Hotel doing the same. This is because of his concern for the environment and not because of his salary level as his boss has assured me. He was being paid what he was worth, I was told.

Finally, he made his single, most important contribution to his department. He left it! He left it Ladies and Gentlemen, to take up the most demeaning job in the company. He now works in that department we all know is inherently evil. What can you say about a man who gives up his most important asset to join this group? Namely his brains. Yes, he has left his brains in his previous department but has given all his other parts to the new department.

And now, as his career has bottomed out, we can expect Doug to rise again and serve the people, because he belongs up there. With Einstein, David Suzuki, Harley Davidson and Norton. Yes, Doug is the greatest... don't let his wife, kids and his boss tell you otherwise.

June 1986

Where Have All the Leaders Gone?

What words of wisdom can I give you today?

Some of you may have seen the play *'Fiddler on the Roof'*. In one scene of the play, the rabbi was asked by his persecuted followers: "Rabbi, rabbi. Is there a blessing for the czar?"

The rabbi thought a little bit and answered. "Yes, there is. May the Good Lord bless and keep the czar. Far away from us..."

That was a good answer. The czar was not a desirable leader and his remoteness would be appreciated. I'm not sure if I have any easy answers for you today about leadership. Although you've been asking me many questions over the years. However, it is especially important to address you today, not as your principal, but more as a good friend.

This year may have been confusing to many of you because it appeared that all basic concepts of leadership and decency had been violated during 1989. Some of you may have lost faith in leadership, you certainly may have lost trust. And this is what I want to discuss with you today. And the question: 'Where have all the leaders gone?'

On your graduation today, you are at the doorway to a whole new world. You are about to open the door to entirely different experiences. You have spent many years been taught subjects such as Science, Mathematics and Humanities. And some of you may even have found some of this to be relevant.

But now it is time to go out into the world. Some of you will perhaps seek further punishment in university. Others will try to make a living but don't know where to start. And you want some guidance. You look to others to lead you into the unknown. To boldly go where many mediocre people have gone before. Out there, in some nondescript job for some struggling oil company, climbing the ladder of success, and then having problems managing, since you may not be fully prepared.

I was in the same position many years ago, graduating, and then not knowing what to do. Here I was at the gates of the school armed with a diploma but not knowing what I was to do next. I needed the answers. I had many questions but had little guidance because I was naïve and confused.

Throughout my school years I had been looking for someone to emulate. Some were athletes, characters in movies, or someone I had read about in a novel or magazine. People such as a Rafer Johnson a Decathlon winner, or the dashing and debonair, John F. Kennedy. It was important to me that I always had a symbol to set my sights on, somewhat like a captain on an old-time sailing ship, setting his sight on a distant lighthouse when the seas get rough.

Growing up can be a rough experience. We feel our parents have let us down, have not given us the time, nor the guidance, that we expect them to. They do not understand the problems and, what little they communicate with us, only raises more questions to be answered. They punish us when we don't deserve to be punished. And then, parents can be so boring and so predictable. They try to impose values on us that are from a generation that you could never communicate with in the first place. They set the standards that they weren't able to achieve themselves, when they were our age. Yet they expect us to achieve, to excel and to make them proud of a product that they spend so little time in molding.

Where were they during our first Christmas concert? We were proud of those wings. Where were they when our team won the big game? We needed them to share the joy, but they weren't there...

Perhaps we expect too much of our parents. Perhaps we don't realize that they are no different than we are, in our feelings. They need us too, and they need someone to guide them. They cannot be leaders. Can they?

So then, where are our leaders?

We had a television preacher who, for many years, guided our morals like so many television personalities do. Today he is in jail.

We have an orphanage where many homeless children went for protection, but instead received abuse and torture in their innocent years. Torture by people whom they were supposed to trust. Today these people are being questioned.

Where are our leaders?

We have had hockey stars who thousands of children look up to, who are now facing charges of drunken driving, assault and battery and public misconduct.

We have seen judges in Manitoba been relieved of their duties for compromising the law. And they told us our judicial system was second to none...

Are these our role models?

Where our leaders?

We have seen parents abandon their own children because they cannot communicate with each other, except through a lawyer.

Where are our leaders?

And is this what is to become of you when you go out into the world? The answer is "no". Unbelievable isn't it? No?

How can I say that? Quite easily, I'll say it again "no".

Don't be discouraged by what you perceive as the lack of leadership in today's society. Be encouraged instead that in your time these events are being reported and debated rather than being concealed, as they were in the good old days. Things have become much better through the years. We have evolved and improved and are much better today, as a society, than during our grandfather's time.

In the 'good old days', children were working twelve hours a day in the filthy factories of London and Dublin.

Today child labour is forbidden in progressive nations.

In the good old days, it was common to beat your wife regularly and get away with it. Not anymore. More and more women are finding public support and protection from the criminals they are married to.

And in the good old days parents had tremendous power over their children and could beat them. These were considered as good parents who felt that corporal punishment was the only way to discipline children. Show them who to fear. Show them who's the boss. Show them the awesome power parents had. And show them how few brains they had...

Does discipline mean brutality?

Does discipline mean controlling by fear?

Not anymore. Not today.

Today these criminals are being brought to justice and that is good. Charges could never have been laid at the Mount Cashel orphanage thirty years ago.

Things are getting better today.

We have found criminals in the robes of a judge and the uniform of police officers, among the evangelists, and hidden behind the cloth. And today we are bringing them to justice. Something that was never even contemplated as late as 1970.

There are few heroes and there are few saints. But there are many human beings with a lot of problems. They need your help.

You, as ordinary human beings, can help them. You can be a leader. You can set the example and set the standards. Leadership by example has always been the most effective type of leadership.

Image is so important in leadership. Perhaps so important that it detracts from the substance of leadership. Woe is the politician who appears on television with an unkempt appearance. The masses immediately reject him, or her. Did you know that the Press is not allowed to take photographs of Queen Elizabeth as she is in the process of eating? They can't do that because she is supposed to be 'God-like'. And if the masses saw her eating to sustain herself, they would be confused. 'This is not normal' they would say. She probably puts on her gloves one at a time, just like us. Just like us. That is so important. Just like us...

The leaders are just like us. If only they could walk with us, talk with us, they would comprehend and we would understand that they alone cannot solve the world's problems. They need us, and we need them.

You are the only leader that is important. If you can look into the mirror and believe in yourself, you do not need those heroes, idols and royalty to guide you.

If you can satisfy yourself that what you are doing is something vital, then you are a hero in your little world.

Too much emphasis is put on winning. Hundreds of books have been written on the subject and many deal with it in a very superficial way. It is not essential to win. It is essential to achieve. To achieve your self esteem and self respect and look the world in the eye and tell the world you gave it your best shot.

You are not necessarily the most intelligent in your class, perhaps you got mediocre grades. But if you can convince yourself that the mediocre grades you received were the maximum you were capable off at that time, with the time and tools that you had, then that is sufficient.

You do not have to convince others. If you convince yourself, others will be convinced.

Far too much emphasis is put in winning and keeping up with the great achievers. When the stock market crashed a few times, some of us read that the 'winners' jumped off buildings. They jumped off because they couldn't cope with the reality of the temporary loss of self esteem.

When I was in university some students committed suicide, or took pills because they could not cope with the stress of staying abreast with the winners. They refused to accept their limitations. Some believed they didn't have any. Some believed they were meant to fly and they come crashing down to earth.

Winning is nice, you get the admiration and respect of others. You're up there, with the greatest...

But are you the greatest?

What words of wisdom can I give you as you leave this hall?

Not much.

You do not need anyone to preach to you. You are old enough to know right from wrong and that is the most important. You will all succeed, by your own definition. You will all be what you want to be, if you feel that is what you want to be.

Some of you will want to become the Prime Minister, but will you really be happy if you had a job like Brian Mulroney's? Many of you will find considerable challenge in what may appear to be humble jobs. I feel that there's no such thing as a humble job. You can be a king in any job. Percy Pegler had a school named after him in Okotoks. He was the Caretaker. Everyone loved him and he was a king.

When you go out into the working world, don't expect others to set the example. People try, but often fail. Understand that we often fail, because we are human.

So, where all the leaders?

They are here. Within us. You are the leaders. You are the role models for your younger brothers and sisters, your friends and, in the future, for your children.

You must lead by your good example.

You will have many opportunities to compromise your values and your principles, and occasionally you may give in. Pull yourself out of it, as the next generation is watching you.

Watching what you do. Watching and learning. You are no longer the student. You are the teacher. You are the leader. Your world is waiting for you. Good luck.

November 1989

A Mishap at a Hot and Steamy Place

The Laundromat is a great place to socialize. All kinds of people go there. Rich people, poor people, young and old. It's just a beehive of activity and there is never a dull moment in a Laundromat. The gossip at this place could never be read about in the *National Enquirer*. Would probably be rejected due to poor taste...

If you want peace and quiet, you could visit one at closing time and watch the Spin Dryer. It's more fun than watching Lawrence Welk...

I know several people that have expensive washers and dryers in their homes, who still go to Laundromats to meet with new people and gossip about their neighbours. Then there are perverts who show up just to look at the latest in a women's underwear. I'm not that kind of person. But I'm partial to high heels. Because I'm short.

There are others who use it as a babysitting service and leave screaming kids while they go shopping across the street, assuming that the others in the Laundromat will look after them, and only come back to find that an irate customer put them into the Spin Dryer. *'But I was only taking him for a spin!'*

And then there are some finicky house wives who like to prove that the detergent they use gives the cleanest wash in town. There are also the health nuts who claim that only the hot water in the commercial washer will kill all the bacteria resident in their underwear.

And so on, and so on... There are still a lot of reasons to visit the Laundromat. So, take a friend to the Laundromat this weekend. It's the hottest entertainment in town. And it's cheap too. But the experience I had in 1974 was a memorable one.

I had just graduated from university and my first job was in Toronto. I had $50.00 in my pocket and had found a decrepit apartment on Yonge Street. (They should roll up Yonge Street and put it in a washer). The decrepit apartment I was staying in didn't have laundry facilities. So, one Saturday night, when I didn't have a date, which was usually the case, (nobody liked me), I decided to do my laundry. You never know who you may meet in that hot and steamy place. Could get into a lot of hot water though. But it's good clean fun, which my mother always recommended to me.

So, I walked into the Laundromat. '*All you can wash for 25¢. Hot water 5¢ extra*'.

The place had only one woman sitting on a green, plastic chair, with rollers in her hair, reading the *National Enquirer*. I had a copy to... The headline that day was '*Old Woman Gives Birth to a Monkey.*' I couldn't wait to read it...

I held my breath and opened my green garbage bag. Five pairs of socks, six pieces of underwear, five shirts, four towels, a pair of jeans, black lace underwear... (I remember her well). One cup of detergent, a quarter and a nickel for a hot water and the machine sprang to life.

I settled back on a green plastic chair and began reading about the dear old woman. I had got to the part when the monkey had grown up and found a career as a politician, when suddenly my laundry tub stopped agitating. The other woman's machine was fine, so how come mine came to a stop? Could it be a case of rejection? I mean, my clothes were not that dirty...

I opened the cover of the tub which was filled to the brim with scalding water. I shook the machine. Nothing happened... I kicked it, the woman's eyebrows shot up. I pushed the coin feeder in and out several times. Nothing. Put in another quarter and a nickel. Nothing.

I looked around for something to fish out my clothes with. Nothing could be seen.

This was a serious crisis. What was I going to wear for the next month or two? Oh no!

"Can you suggest something?" I asked the Roller Derby Queen, but she shrugged her shoulders and carried on reading the *National Enquirer*.

I looked outside on the sidewalk for some sticks to fish out my clothes, but there were none. Panic set in. What was I to do?

Leonardo would probably come in soon and fish out my stuff and put it into the garbage thinking these were just rags. I ran back to the apartment and all I could find were two wooden spoons. I rushed back to the Laundromat and plunged the spoons into the scalding brew. The Roller Derby Queen burst out laughing. I mean, what's so funny about me digging into the laundry tub with wooden spoons? I could have been cooking split pee soup!

Finally, after considerable stirring and fishing, despite the hysterical laughter from my friend in rollers, I was able to get my clothes out. But alas! My favorite pair of jeans was missing. I plunged my spoons in again. No luck. I stirred the cauldron several times. Nothing.

Where could my jeans have gone? Could they have dissolved?

I finally gave up and dragged the heavy, dripping garbage bag back to the apartment. But then I suspected that the Roller Derby Queen probably stole them. I dashed back but she was gone, along with her copy of the *National Enquirer*.

Whenever I hear that song *Jean, Jean,* tears come to my eyes because that was my favourite pair. I miss that pair a lot. It took years to break them in.

So, if you ever visit Toronto and see a woman with rollers in her hair, reading *The National Enquirer,* wearing a pair of jeans with two patches on the rump and two on the knees, who you gonna call?

April 1990

Made in the USA
San Bernardino, CA
21 September 2018